Also by Florence Waszkelewicz Clowes:

- Pol-Am, A History of the Polish Americans in Pittsfield, MA 1862-1945.

- Bones in the Backyard, a Bashia Gordon Mystery with Lois Blackburn

- Old Secrets Never Die, a Bashia Gordon Mystery with Lois Blackburn

POLISH FOLK LEGENDS

RETOLD BY
FLORENCE WASZKELEWICZ CLOWES

ILLUSTRATED BY
DANIEL HASKIN

To my mother, Sophie,
who never doubted me,
and my children,
Jim, Jerry, Sue, Pat and Sandy,
who had to endure me.

POLISH
FOLK
LEGENDS

RETOLD BY
FLORENCE
WASZKELEWICZ CLOWES

ILLUSTRATED BY
DANIEL HASKIN

Copyright © 1992, 1993, 2004 by Florence Waszkelewicz Clowes
Revised Edition 2010

ISBN 0-7414-5840-3

Printed in the United States of America

Published March 2010

INFINITY PUBLISHING
1094 New DeHaven Street, Suite 100
West Conshohocken, PA 19428-2713
Toll-free (877) BUY BOOK
Local Phone (610) 941-9999
Fax (610) 941-9959
Info@buybooksontheweb.com
www.buybooksontheweb.com

ACKNOWLEDGEMENTS

I have had the good fortune to prepare this revised edition for publication with my editor, Jon Jansen, whose competence helped shape the book and whose patience made the whole process seemingly effortless.

My heartfelt gratitude to Mark Kohan, editor of the *Polish American Journal*, who published the first and second editions. Also to the many people in the United States and Poland who contributed to this collection. Without their encouragement, this book of Legends would not have been published.

ABOUT THE AUTHOR

Florence Waszkelewicz Clowes has been published in many periodicals and is book review editor for the *Polish American Journal*. Her books include *POL-AM, Polish Americans in Pittsfield MA.*, and *Bones in the Backyard, a Bashia Gordon Mystery* and *Old Secrets Never Die* with Lois Blackburn. Clowes lives in Vero Beach, Florida.

ABOUT THE ILLUSTRATOR

Daniel Haskin is a professional web site designer, artist and illustrator for his company, Data Design Group. His work has been exhibited in western New York and Canada as well as the *Buffalo News* and the *Polish American Journal*. He lives in Kenmore, New York.

FOREWORD

Many of us can recall the joy of sitting on a parent's or grandparent's knee and listening with full attention to their account of a gallant knight's battle with a dragon, a soaring carpet or an unsightly duckling.

These tales, passed from generation to generation, are part of a folk tradition centuries-old. They come from a culture that knows neither a particular place nor time, other than far away and long ago. Woven in a colorful fabric of myth and lore, they praise the simple truths of life.

Today, many of us long for the simple life. After balancing schedules, paying bills, cleaning the house, taking the kids to baseball practice and what not, it is comforting to know the prince does marry the princess, and the emperor was a fool after all.

One way hundreds of thousands of Americans seek the simpler life is by studying the ways of their ancestors. Besides the genealogical questions of how, why and when they came to this great country, we want to know what they ate, what they sang, and what stories they told their children.

Their values are given to us in their culture. Our ancestors' art, music, prose and poetry speaks louder than any volume of research that could be found.

While *Polish Folk Legends* is designed to give us a sampling of the legends of Poland, the stories within are as enchanting and alluring as the classics we learned as children. You will ride alongside kings and saints, travel deep into mines, and take part in harvest celebrations.

You will also learn of folklore that is unique to Poland—fabled storks, the man in the moon, and the trumpeter whose haunting unfinished call-to-arms is still acknowledged to this day.

The *Polish-American Journal* which published the first and second printing of the Polish Folk Legends is pleased to see this revised edition of these timeless legends. Clowes' technique is simply golden. It will gladden your heart and the hearts of all who read the book.

Mark A. Kohan
Editor in Chief
Polish-American Journal

INTRODUCTION

In 1975, while attending a Summer Ethnology Course in Kielce, Poland, I became fascinated with folklore and began collecting folk legends. The more I collected, the more I learned and laughed about my heritage.

Early ethnologists such as Marcin Bielski, Jan Dlugosz, Vincent Kadlubek, Ignacy Krasicki, Wladyslaw Wociecki and Zorian Chodakowski copied down the oral tales, legends, songs and traditions, providing me with a wealth of material to draw from.

Folklore, according to Professor Jozef Burszta of Poznan, reflects the nation's traditional culture, an anonymous sum-total of a people's oral traditions and legends, their poetry, songs, music, art, religious beliefs and customs. He had edited a 70 volume collection, *The Complete Works of Oskar Kolberg*, the great nineteenth Century ethnologist. Kolberg, alone, collected an entire body of knowledge of Polish folk culture, comprised of 12,500 songs, 1,250 legends, 670 tales, 2,700 proverbs, and 370 puzzles.

I have chosen to concentrate on one type of folklore—legends. Legends, more than any other type of tale, have a basis of truth in their premise. They are sometimes referred to as folk history. They reflect the nation's dreams and passions, its sins and virtues. A nation without legends would be lacking in fullness, for it is in legend that the collective imagination is reflected.

Ethnologists have categorized legends into four groups, on the basis of their primary concern. Professor Julian Krzyzanowski uses this grouping in his *The Systematic Catalog of the Polish Folktale*. While this book is not a scholarly book, I have chosen to use this grouping for my collection of legends. A commentary follows each legend, providing information pertaining to location, event or person involved.

The four groups consist of the following:
1. Religious
    a. Stories of lives of Christian saints.
    b. Traditional stories of miracles, revelations, icons, blessings and so on.
    c. Biblical narratives that have been expanded.
2. Supernatural
    a. Factual accounts of occurrences and experiences which seem to support superstitions.
    b. A narrative of a personal happening, but traditional in content.
    c. Supernatural creatures—elves, magic, ghosts, evil and good.
       Gives credence to folk beliefs, cures and wishes that come true.
3. Personal
    a. Stories attached to individuals and told as truth. Hero legends.
4. Historical and Local
    a. Closely associated with a specific place.
    b. Semi-historical events, reflecting the character of the nation.

Sources used for these legends often contained a differentiation in spelling and accent marks. No orthographic symbols or accents have been used in this book.

If readers enjoy this collection, gain a broader understanding of the character of the Polish people, and learn a little more of the history and geography of the country, I feel my efforts will have been successful.

Florence Waszkelewicz Clowes

Contents

PoLSKA

LEGEND OF THE GOLDEN DUCK

Long, long ago there was a poor boy named Kasmierz, who lived in Warsaw. He often sat and listened to his babcia and dziadzio tell tales of the kings and queens of Poland.

"Kaz," they would say, "there is a great treasure still buried in the cellars of the castle on the Vistula." And they would go on to tell him about the treasure that was guarded by the Golden Duck and the many brave men that tried to find the fortune. None of them could outsmart the Duck.

Kaz was poor and nothing interested him more than the treasure, for he could think of all the things he would do with the gold. He never bought new clothes and there was no money for toys— Dziadzio made his toys. There never was enough money for anything but food. Kaz decided he would find the treasure, so he would be able to have all these things.

Off he went. In the dark dungeons under the castle he lit a candle. In the dim light, he wandered through the tunnels a long time, searching dark corners for signs of a hidden treasure.

Suddenly, he came to an underground lake. The candlelight on the water made it look like a great silver coin. And in the lake there swam a Golden Duck. Kaz stood still, fascinated by the scene.

The duck swam close to where Kaz stood and when he spoke the lake lit up, bright as day. The light blinded him and he shielded his eyes with his hand.

"So, you seek my treasure!'' said the Golden Duck. "Well, I'll make a bargain with you. I'll give you a sack of gold, if you can spend it all on yourself in a single day, without giving a penny to another soul, all the riches and treasures buried in this lake will be yours."

Well, Kaz thought that was a fine task and he agreed. In a wink of an eye, he was back on the streets of Warsaw. And he lived like a King for the whole day. He bought himself beautiful clothes, a horse and carriage made of pure gold. He even bought a castle. But he liked the horse best and spent a good deal of time riding about the city. When at last he jumped off his horse, he began to look around for more things to spend his gold on, for he still had a few more coins left.

A little orphan came by, ragged and dirty, begging for bread. When he saw the King Kaz, he begged all the more and cried out loud, "Please, kind Sir, give me a coin so I might buy bread for my family."

Kaz felt sorry for the child and reached into his pocket and gave him a coin. He forgot all about the bargain he made with the Golden Duck.

Suddenly the whole street trembled and shook. It thundered and a clap of lightning struck Kaz. All his fine clothing disappeared, so did the horse and carriage. He lost his riches and was left as he started—a poor boy.

He never was able to find the silver lake under the castles of Warsaw, nor the Golden Duck who guarded the money and as far as I know, neither has anyone else. They gave up looking for the Duck, even though the same street is still there. It is called Tamka. And the old castle is still there, waiting for you to search for the hidden treasure.

babcia and dziadzio—grandma and grandpa.

TREASURES, INDEED, *are to be found in the deep re-cesses of castles in Poland. The crypts of kings, queens and bishops beneath the floors contain priceless relics in gold and silver and jewels. Today they are carefully guarded and not by a duck. The recent plunder of St. Wojciech's in Poznan is a warning of the persistence of treasure seekers.*

THE ROBBER'S DANCE

Once there were great dense forests in Podhale. And many men lived there. Some called them outlaws, robbers and highwaymen who robbed for a living. Some say they were bad, others say they were only living by their wits and besides, they often gave their booty to the poor, of which there were many.

Janosik was one of these men who lived in the mountain passes. He was famous for his feats of daring, not only in robbing the rich but in his dancing and high-jumping. The other men tried to compete with him but there was no catching up with Janosik. Sitting about the campfire at night, the men would recount the day's events, tell tales and sing songs. They would hold contests in seeing who could jump highest over the flames of the bonfire but no one could match Janosik's skill.

One day, however, a jealous girlfriend disclosed his whereabouts to the local authorities and before you knew it, he was arrested. A quick trial followed and he was condemned to death by hanging.

Janosik wasn't ashamed of his deeds, for he looked upon them as an act against the oppressive authorities and he took his sentence bravely. While he waited for the scaffold to be built, he asked his jailers if he might dance once again.

Dancers like him were no common turnip and everyone knew what a good show he would put on. The judges consented.

He was brought into the courtroom, which had a large open floor. People crowded into the balcony, anxious and sad, to see this last great exhibition. Janosik danced. He whirled, he twirled, he leapt. Now he was in the air, then down on one knee. He struck the floor with a rhythmic heel. He marked the measure with little staccato whoops. He twinkled his feet and touched the rafters with his head. That was the way Janosik danced.

The dance was reaching its climax. The people cheered and shouted with delight at each feat. The guards tapped their toes, forgetting their duties. Suddenly Janosik made a great bound, greater than any other. He went flying across the room and out the window. Out he went, as clean as an arrow and no one ever saw him again.

Podhale—a mountainous region in southeast Poland

ROBBER THEMES *dominate the Podhale paintings on glass—the brigands dancing or carrying kettles full of gold. The pictures give excellent examples of dress, weapons and accessories of the styles in those times. Colors, unlike those in the central plains, were dark, as a rule. The art of reverse painting on glass was an accomplishment in itself, as any modern artist knows.*

The rob-the-rich and give-to-the-poor theme of highway robbers is known throughout Europe and England, the most famous being Robin Hood. Tales and legends of the Podhale robbers are kept alive through the Podhale Society in Zakopane, who also conduct highlander dialect language courses for the benefit of its members.

ZWYRTALA, THE VILLAGE FIDDLER

Old Zwyrtala died one night and went to heaven, his fiddle still under his arm. The gates were closed. He didn't want to ring the bell and waken everyone, so he sat down and waited. Soon he got bored and tightening the pegs of his fiddle, he began to play, ever so softly. But gradually it grew louder and as he thought of the wife he had left on earth, he began to sing:

Praise be to the bachelor's life
Wherever I look, everywhere my wife.

Suddenly, a voice called: "Who's there?"
That must be Saint Peter, thought Zwyrtala.
"Me," he called.
"Who—me?"
"Zwyrtala."
"Why are you yelling?"
"I'm not yelling, I'm singing!"
"The dev—", Saint Peter broke off, "with such singing! And why did you come so late?"
"Well, I died just after supper."
"After supper? You should only be halfway here by now."
"E-e-y Saint Peter, I'm a quick one. I'm from the highlands!"
"Well, now. . . sit there until daylight and don't make so much noise!"
Zwyrtala sat quietly and when the morning began to dawn, he picked up his fiddle and began playing. A head peeped out from behind the gates, then a second and then a third. Angels.
"Oh, oh, listen how he plays," said one.

11

When Zwyrtala heard that, he struck up a march at once, on all four strings.

"Ah, how beautiful it is!" exclaimed one of the angels. "What music is that?"

"That's the 'Robbers' March,' " he answered.

"Ah, the 'Robbers' March!' "

They began to call the other angels and clap their hands to the music. How beautiful the sounds were.

Just then, a key turned in the lock and the gates of heaven were opened. Saint Peter stepped outside.

"Zwyrtala!"

"Yes?"

"Come along."

"I don't need to be asked twice into Heaven!"

Already it was known all over Heaven that there was a Highlander with his fiddle. The news had reached Pan Bog Himself, who was sitting on the porch smoking his pipe. He wasn't doing anything today because it was Sunday. He sent one of the angels, not a little one with a white gown and white wings but a tall one with silver armor and rainbow wings and flaming sword, to fetch Zwyrtala.

The angel found Zwyrtala getting assigned to his quarters.

"Is it true you know how to play?" he asked.

"It's true."

"The Robber's tune?"

"Yes."

"Will you play it for Pan Bog?"

"Of course," he answered. And away they went, through a broad street with silver houses on each side, with saints sitting outside. Finally, they came to one made of gold and there was Pan Bog on the porch. Zwyrtala made a deep bow and Pan Bog nodded his head and waved his hand.

"Play."

So Zwyrtala tuned up and drew his bow to the last hair.

Hey my darling, Janecko
Tell me where'd that feather go that I gave you.
To the war I had to go and lost it where the waters
flow, my love.

And so on, to the very end. Pan Bog was very pleased. All the saints and angels and the elect had gathered around to listen and I tell you, they couldn't praise Zwyrtala enough for his playing. He was so happy that his hair stood on end. The saints begged the Highlander to go on.

He burst into song:

When I let out a song from my high mountain perch,
it sounds like the organ playing in church.

Everyone clapped in delight. "How beautiful, how lovely!"

And so it went, Zwyrtala playing and singing and whatnot. Everyone was joining in. When Saint Joseph came along, he heard the little girl angels singing:

When I was a baby in a bib,
The boys came crowding 'round my crib.

He listened some more and heard the deep boy angel voices:

If you won't become one of my family, say, I'll kill
the rapscallion that stands in my way.

This was scarcely finished when Saint Joseph heard the whole angel choir singing so loudly, it resounded throughout the entire Heaven:

Lord, beat that shepherd who leads his sheep. . .

That was too much for Saint Joseph. He held his head in his hands. "What have we come to?" He rushed to Saint Peter.

13

Saint Peter was in the place where the Angelic Host always held their choir practice. Instead of Archangel Gabriel with his golden baton and trumpet, Zwyrtala sat on a chair playing his fiddle. All around him were the angels and elect rehearsing the Robbers' tune.

"Good Lord!" cried Saint Joseph. "What's going on here?"

Just then the Archangel came along and said that nobody wanted to sing anything but mountain songs anymore—even Saint Cecilia. Zwyrtala was teaching them, he added. "Extraordinary things!"

Night came and from every corner could be heard snatches of Highland song. All Heaven was in an uproar. In the morning, Saint Peter said to the Archangel Gabriel, "Hadn't we better call Zwyrtala?"

"Well, all right."

Zwyrtala came, fiddle under his arm and bowed before them.

"Zwyrtala, couldn't you go somewhere else?" asked Saint Peter.

"Leave here?"

"Yes."

"Away from Heaven?"

"Aha."

"Where to?"

"Aha. Where to? That's just it." Saint Peter thought for awhile.

"And what for?" demanded Zwyrtala. "They sent me here when I died."

"Yes, exactly."

"I didn't steal, I didn't kill, I didn't fight."

"I know, I know."

"Well, then, what?"

"Well, everyone in Heaven is singing Highlandish ever since you came. They had a new song to learn for the Holiday. Instead, they learned yours."

"E-e-y, so that's it."

"Zwyrtala," said Saint Peter. He paused. "Where do you want to go?"

He scratched his head before answering. "I know where to go."

"Where?"

"Where I came from."

"On earth?"

"That's it."

"I was thinking of sending you to some star!"

"Don't bother. I'll go down below."

"From Heaven."

"That will be Heaven for me. I'll just play in the woods and valleys. I'll never let the old music die out. Soft-like, I'll play to the boy guarding the sheep. I'll sing to the little one with her cows in the Uplands. When the old farmer comes along to the forest, I'll play in his ears, as our fathers used to play and when nobody's there, I'll have the water in the stream and the wind whistling through the trees. I won't be lonely and I won't miss Heaven.

"When I was living, I sometimes used to ask Pan Bog if he wouldn't let me stay here forever in the Highlands and now my wish is granted."

"Well, Zwyrtala, go along then, for here you are Highlandizing the whole place! You won't miss Heaven?"

"Heaven is where my heart is," and with that he made a very nice bow and passed through the heavenly gates onto the road leading down to Earth. It was night and down the Milky Way he went, carrying his fiddle under his arm. When he knew he was alone, he danced along, singing a tune:

A Highlander I'll be, the Tatras my domain, On the high winds I'm cradled and refreshed in the rain.

He went on singing his song along the Milky Way until he came to the summit of a rocky peak and there he entered into the deep valley of the Tatras.

If you ever go into the Highlands, listen for his song!

Pan Bog—God.

KAZIMIERZ TETMAJER (1865-1940), *a native of the Tatra foothills, is most famous as a poet but he also helped preserve the oral traditions of the old mountaineers and bygone epics of valiant mountain bandits in his* Na Skalnym Podhalu *(In the Rocky Highlands), from which this tale is taken.*

The Podhale Valley is an ethnographically distinct region, enclosed by the Danajec River in the North and the Tatra Mountains in the south. Zakopane is perhaps the most famous town in this very southern tip of Poland.

Settled by migrating nomadic tribes from Transylvania in the 16th Century, its people have retained a strong attachment to their music, customs, folklore and dress. An elongated type of instrument, the zlabcoki, *was used universally by the Highlander musicians until the 19th Century, when it gave way to the standard violin.*

The Podhale people are known for their extraordinary vim and vigor, as demonstrated by the leg motions and high leaps in the air during the men's zbojnicki *dance. Their traditional dress of white trousers made of thick, homespun wool and embroideries in the beautiful parzanica pattern, the broad leather belt with bronze clasps, the white linen shirt and round black hat, is perhaps one of the most famous outfits in the world.*

Polish Folk Legends

THE FERN BLOSSOM

Once there was a small boy named Jacus who lived in a small village near a large forest. It was St. John's Eve and many of his friends had started to build a huge bonfire for the evening but he didn't join them. He had heard about the wallfern that blossomed only on that one day and decided that this year he would go and look for it. There were magical powers for whoever found it—riches, happiness, popularity—and he was determined to be the one to receive such luck!

It was dark and scary in the forest, thick with trees, bushes and vines. But Jacus was determined and wriggled through trees on small animal paths. After a while he noticed a light in the distance and headed straight for it. The twinkling light seem to be like a star, hovering over something. When he arrived to the place where the light glittered, it looked like a pale flame but nothing nearby was burned or caught fire. Then he realized he had found the wallfern, the flower with magic, that lit the area bright as day!

He reached down to pick it, almost afraid of getting burned. But the star-shaped flower only felt cool in his hand. Suddenly he heard a voice.

"You are a lucky young man, now that you have me!"

Jacus looked around but could see nothing beyond the circle of light. The voice spoke again. It seemed to come from the flower!

"You will have all your wishes come true for the rest of your life! Only one thing—you must agree not to share your luck with anyone else!"

Jacus thought, "How strange! Who is talking? Why would I want to share this fortune with anyone?"

He only nodded his head in agreement and, clutching the flower, headed for home. Making his way out of the forest, he began to think of all the things he wanted—nice clothes, riches and jewels, a new cottage—no, a huge palace, with servants all about!

At the edge of the forest he looked about, confused. It was a strange place! He stood in a magnificent courtyard, in a new outfit of the best cloth. His shoes had golden heels, his belt was covered with fine jewels and his shirt was made of the finest linen. A coach stood by, with six white horses with golden collars and servants stood ready to wait on him as he explored the beauty of the castle.

That was the beginning of Jacus's luck and he became a fine prince, enjoying all his luxury. As time went on, he wondered what had become of his parents and his little village back home. He had everything he desired but kept wondering how they were doing.

One day, he finally decided to do something about it and got into the coach and wished himself to his parent's home.

Everything was just as he had left it a few years ago but there was no one at the door. A beggar standing nearby asked him, "Why is a fine gentleman like you looking at a place like this? The house is empty. Everyone died of poverty, hunger and disease!"

"It was my fault that they died!" Jacus" said. "I want to die, too! I can't live this way any longer!"

He had hardly finished talking when the earth opened up underneath him and he disappeared, the magical wallfern blossom with him, which is why it can no longer be found!

ACCORDING TO OLD SLAVIC LEGENDS, *strange things happen on St. John's Eve. Animals talk, the earth reveals its underground secrets, plants take on magical properties, devils and witches command unusual powers and the wallfern blooms at midnight with a flaming flower. Fortune and happiness will come to anyone who finds it but it is difficult to find and is guarded by demonic figures.*

St. John's Day, June 24th, the longest day of the year, marks the peak of summer. St. John has a special attraction to youth, love and fertility. Fire and water are also two important elements. A new fire must be started on this eve to ward off misfortune, lightning and sickness and to encourage successful marriages, Young people spend the evening playing games, leaping over the bonfire and sometimes running into the water.

Water, an important element in the agricultural life, was seen as a purifier. Young girls cast flower-wreaths, lit with candles on them on the water and watch the course they take down the river. Boys would dart into the water, or with long sticks retrieve the wreaths, which might have the result of courtship and marriage with its maker.

People at the seashore would sprinkle their boats with holy water and lay branches of herbs and grasses, that were blessed on Corpus Christi, in the bottoms of their boats or intertwine them in their fishnets. This was done to ward off evil powers that caused terrible winds, rough seas and tangled nets.

Songs of St. John's Eve are associated with wedding songs, as befitting a saint who specializes in love and fertility.

The leaves are falling all around, all around,
Time for you, young farmer,
To seek you a wife, seek you a wife. . .

PAN TWARDOWSKI

Twardowski was a curious nobleman. He wanted to know everything there was to know. He studied the sciences and became a doctor, where he hoped to learn how to live forever. In an old book he read how one was able to call up the Devil and after many attempts, the Devil appeared before him.

"What is it you want?" the Devil asked. "Why have you called me from the underworld?"

"I want to know how to live forever," Twardowski said. "I want to know everything, to be rich and have everything I wish."

"That's a big order," declared the Devil. "What will you give me in return?"

Twardowski said nothing and the Devil continued.

"I will give you anything you ask for, if you will give me your soul."

Twardowski had heard about this and he wondered. What would it really matter if he traded his soul for all the things he wanted. What would it really matter, he thought.

The Devil was anxious to draw up a contract. He didn't want this soul to get away. "We can sign a pact in blood," he said. "Remember, your wishes will be fulfilled and some day in the future, I get your soul."

"How do I know you can do all the things you say you can do?"

"Why, test me."

"All right, let's see if you can fly over all of Poland and collect all the silver in the land and deposit it at Olkusz in one night."

With a great whirlwind the Devil was gone. The next day,

Twardowski decided to travel to Olkusz. Sure enough, there in the region were mounds of silver. And the Devil stood nearby. "Well, how's that trick for you?" he asked.

Twardowski was impressed all right, but he wasn't quite sure he wanted to sell his soul for a mound of silver. "I think you better prove yourself again," he said.

"What is it this time, then?"

"If I am going to know all things, I have to get about the countryside as fast as you. You will have to get me some transportation that will take me anywhere I want to go. Through the air, over water and land, quick as a wink!"

"Is that all?" laughed the Devil. (At that Twardowski quickly made up his mind to demand yet another test.) "Come with me." The Devil whirled Twardowski to a house in Krakow that had an enormous weathervane in the shape of rooster. It was a beautiful rooster, plump and painted red, with a fine flowing comb.

"Mount! Fly!" cried the Devil and before Twardowski knew it, he was on the rooster, flying over the rooftops to go here and there, and they went quicker than the wind. Finally, Twardowski ordered him home. The rooster landed at the very doorstep of Twardowski's home and vanished into the air before Twardowski could turn around.

The Devil was waiting for him. "How did you like that?" he asked. And then he pulled out a contract. "Come, let's sign this thing. I can see how much you enjoy your newfound treasures!"

But Twardowski hesitated. "One more test—can you make a rope of sand and pull up that tree with it?"

Well, the Devil was more than a little concerned about that task but he said nothing and flew into the air to the banks of the Vistula where there was a wide strip of sand. He scooped up the sand with his hands and nimbly shaped the grains into a rope. Longer and longer it grew. In a twinkling, the rope of sand was finished and hurling through the air. It wrapped itself around a large fir tree and with a jerk the tree was out of the ground and dropped at Twardowski's feet. He watched, fascinated and by this time he knew he would give his soul to learn all the tricks of the Devil.

The Devil rubbed his hands and smiled. "All right, then we'll sign the contract, in blood. I'll give you all the wealth and knowledge in the world and you will give me your soul when I ask for it!"

Well, as I told you, Twardowski was already a pretty smart man. All this while he was trying to think of a plan to get all he could and not lose his soul. At last he spoke. "You can have my soul in exchange for wealth, power and knowledge but you can take it in only one place—Rome! If you can't catch me in Rome, the bargain's off and I get to keep my soul, OK?"

The Devil thought for a minute. He knew what Twardowski was up to. He couldn't enter the holy city. But perhaps he could find a way to disguise himself and confuse everyone. He wanted Twardowski's soul so much, he was willing to take the chance.

"Agreed. Rome and only Rome. You'll hand over your soul when I demand it in Rome!"

As they signed the contract in their own blood, Twardowski made a promise to himself never to visit Rome. The Devil snatched the contract and disappeared before a word was spoken.

Twardowski was filled with excitement and decided to test his new powers. He called for his mount and in a twinkle was flying over the Polish land, over rivers and woods, fields and villages. He stopped in Olkusz. The silver mounds were there, alright!

When he returned home, he started using his knowledge to help the poor people of Krakow. As a doctor, he already knew a great deal about healing but now he seemed able to perform miraculous cures. People began to say he had a magic touch in his hands. He would hold séances and conjure up the dead and look into his crystal ball to tell the future. He even discovered the secret of the philosopher's stone!

When he wanted to have a little fun, he would go to the market place and command the pots and pans being sold there to dance. Everyone thought it was great fun to see clay pots dancing in the streets of the Sukiennic!

25

There were many other wonders he created and left on the Polish land. The pond at Knyszyn, Falcon's Rock at Pieskowa Skala and a half-finished castle in the Zamosc area, for instance.

But what he was most interested in was man himself. He wanted to help get rid of disease and poverty and to find the one miracle all men sought: the fountain of youth! He experimented with all types of mixtures and herbs, testing them on himself.

He would have his servant, Maciek, standing by with an antidote should anything go wrong. Then he began to worry about Maciek learning too many of his secrets. And one time, when Maciek seemed to know too much of the procedure, Twardowski turned him into a spider! He ordered Maciek to always stay at his side, ready to serve him but not in the form of a man. Maciek, of course, had no choice!

For many years, Twardowski continued to study medicine, magic and man. He was generous with people, for he lacked nothing and shared what he had with others. Only Maciek who faithfully stayed near his master, remained a spider.

And then, late one night, there was a knock on the door. A disheveled old man stood in the dim light. "Please come to cure my child. He has a fever no one can break. My wife and I are so worried! I know you will be able to help! Please come with me!"

Maciek was in the cobweb in the corner of the doorway and when he saw the stranger he quickly dropped down, blocking the man with his web. But Twardowski brushed the web aside and tucked Maciek into his belt.

He was moved by the man's request and quickly followed him out the door. They climbed into an old wagon pulled by one old horse and started down the streets of Krakow, heading for the gates. They were in the countryside before Twardowski asked where they were going.

"We live in a small village, not far from here," the man replied. "But I have been so worried about my child that I forgot to feed my horse or myself for that matter. Do you mind if we stop at the next tavern for some feed for the horse and a drink for ourselves.''

"Certainly," replied Twardowski. He could see in the dim moonlight that the horse was heaving and sighing and a little drink for the trip wouldn't hurt anyone.

The narrow dirt road wound through the darkened country-side but soon a small light could be seen ahead. "Ah," sighed the man, "we can stop at the tavern ahead."

Twardowski couldn't recognize the tavern or indeed the area that they were in. After all, he had traveled and visited all of Poland—he should recognize the area—but he shrugged it off, blaming it on the darkness. They left the wagon and entered the tavern. It was dimly lit and there were few people inside, it being so late in the evening.

"What place is this?" he asked the innkeeper.

But at that moment the old man threw off his ragged cloak and began jumping up and down. "We are in The Tavern Rome! I have got you, Twardowski! Did you forget about Karczma pod Rzymen?" The Devil laughed and danced with glee, for now he could claim the soul of his victim.

Twardowski could have pulled some of the magic tricks he learned from the Devil himself but he was a man of honor. He would keep his word, now that he was indeed in Rome, he would keep the promise he made to the Devil so long ago.

And so it was that the Devil took Twardowski firmly by the arm and out the door. "Up!" he cried into the dark night and with a whirl of wind, the two were flying through the darkened sky. They were on their way to the Devil's lair—the under-world!

While they were flying off to the ends of the earth, Twardowski began to think about what he had done and felt guilty for defying God. He started to pray for himself and soon he heard Maciek under his belt, praying too. They prayed to the Virgin Mary to ask God's forgiveness and mercy. Of course, Mary heard them both. She was full of sympathy but what could she do, the Devil already had his hands on Twardowski!

As she watched the strange astronauts, she saw the moon, a brightly lit crescent moon. And so, at the Virgin's bidding, the moon tilted. At the very second when Twardowski and the

Devil flew by, the moon straightened up again. There, on the tip of the moon's crest was Twardowski. His cloak was caught in the tip — he had slipped from the grip of the Devil.

The Devil was flying so fast that it was quite a while before he realized he had lost his victim. Now it was the moon that had Twardowski in its power and the moon was a servant of the Virgin Mary.

Twardowski righted himself and got comfortable on the very tip that rescued him from the Devil. He straightened his cloak and hat and loosened his belt. It was then that Maciek crawled out of his hiding place.

"I knew something was wrong when that old man came to the door. I tried to warn you but you paid no attention. I could not serve you then, how am I to serve you here?" Maciek asked.

"Oh, Maciek, I am so happy you are here! That is service enough. The two of us will live together, while I do penance for having made a pact with the Devil."

And so they lived, between heaven and earth, untroubled by the affairs of men. But once in a while Twardowski wondered what was going on down below and Maciek, the faithful servant, spun a long web-thread to earth and let himself down to gather the news. He travels all over Poland, listening to everything and then climbs back up to his master on the moon.

And even today, or rather tonight, if you look at the moon, I'm sure you will be able to see Pan Twardowski, the Man in the Moon!

THE LEGEND OF PAN TWARDOWSKI *first appears in print in the first part of the 19th Century. It is drawn on the remembrances of a 16th Century magician and perhaps on the writings of Goethe's* Faust. *Faust was a man who supposedly lived from 1480-1538, a sorcerer and magician who claimed to be in league with the devil. He sold his soul to the devil in return for major powers; later, the devil dragged him to hell. Goethe's story contained God's redemption of him in the end.*

Twardowski apparently lived during the time of Zygmunt Augusta. He studied in Germany and Italy. He became a very good doctor and was known to the Bishop of Krakow, Francis Krasinski. He called himself Lawrence Dhur and became a doctor at the royal court of Albert Holenzollern, Prince of Prussia and later was called to Lithuania and the Radziwills.

Some time later, he became connected with the Mniszh brothers, Jerzy and Nicolas, for whom he performed séances and seemingly magical happenings. When the crafts and magic of Twardowski were no longer needed or of interest to the brothers, the doctor was assassinated by their henchmen.

The legend of Twardowski is very popular in Poland and many famous writers have developed the story into ballads and ballet, as well as colorful children's picture books.

Florence Waszkelewicz Clowes

BASILICHEK IN THE VALLEY OF THE DINOSAURS

Long, long ago, in the Polish land, there lived many monsters and wild animals. One monster, a dinosaur—so big!—lived near the settlement of what is now Wilno. He breathed fire and many people called it Basilichek.

Basilichek had a bad habit of destroying the flocks that the shepherds cared for in the fields and breathing fire that scorched and burned the crops but no one could destroy him. The reason for this was because he was so ugly! If anyone tried to fight him, they dropped their head from fright when they saw his ugly, monstrous head.

The villagers were really terrified. Everyone thought about getting rid of the dinosaur but no one was successful. A young boy had an idea.

"Forget it," the villagers cried. "Haven't we tried everything? What do you think you can do? How can you fight an enemy you can't look at?"

Jozef persisted, however. Young boys are like that, you know. They won't listen to their elders. And finally the villagers gave him what he wanted and he was off.

As he neared the cave of Basilichek, he found a place to camp. There he made ready for his experiment, for the boy, although young and brave and stubborn, really didn't know if his idea would work. He took the shield the villagers had given him and started to polish it. It was very large and protected almost all of his body, so there was a lot of rubbing to do. But finally he had the shield so bright and shiny, it was like a mirror.

The next morning he walked to the mouth of the cave. He could see the flames coming from the cave and knew

Basilichek was there and about to come out. When the sun rose, there was a stirring and the great monster started to crawl out of the cave.

Now Jozef trembled. He wondered if there was still time to run away but then he thought of the villagers and how they would laugh. So he quietly crept to the side of the opening and stood his shield at an angle and then hid behind it.

The animal crawled out of the cave and began swinging his tail around when he saw the shiny object. He moved toward it, ready to demolish it, when he suddenly stopped, dead in his tracks! With another mighty roar and groan, he rolled over on his side and died!

Just as Jozef thought, the sight of his ugly face reflected in the shiny shield had been the end of him, just as it had killed so many people in the past!

So above this hill over the cave of Basilichek, the village grew to become the great and lovely city of Wilno, no longer bothered by fire-throwing, ugly monsters.

WHO DARES POO-POO *legends of dragons, monsters and dinosaurs? Not you, I hope! For today Poland still has dinosaurs! In the great Katowice Voivodship Park of Rest and Culture, the Valley of Dinosaurs holds Nemegtosaursus, Saurians, Tar-bososaurs, four-legged Armored Dinosaurs and tiny Pachcephalosaurus.*

These life-size creatures walked this planet hundreds of thousands of years ago and may be the base of many oral legends that passed down from generation to generation, surviving to the present time.

Legends, as well as Paleontology, enables us to view ourselves from the vast expanse of time and perceive our own place in the living world about us, with the continuing evolution of life.

The Valley of Dinosaurs is a popular spot in the park, constructed under the supervision of the Polish Academy of Sciences, Paleontology Institute. The realistic valley, with its collection of dinosaurs in active stances is a favorite of all ages. When next in Katowice, be sure to visit the Park with its Zoo, Children's Playground, Botanical Gardens—and the Valley of the Dinosaurs.

A SMALL RING

Long, long ago a beautiful young princess lived in the land of Hungary. Her father was King of Hungary and he loved her very much. One day the Prince of Poland, Boleslaw Wstydliwy, or The Bashful, saw Kinga and immediately wanted to marry her. They were both very young but the Kings of Poland and Hungary were happy to see them united, for it would strengthen the bonds of friendship between the two countries. And so plans for the wedding began.

Everyone in Hungary loved the young princess, for she was kind and gentle besides being beautiful. They were sorry to see their princess leave. King Bela was sad, also, for it was a long journey by horseback and carriage over mountains and through deep forests to Poland and he would not see her very often.

He wanted to give his daughter a wedding gift she would always treasure and would remember her country by. He gave her great chests of gold and silver as a dowry.

"Daughter," he asked, "What would you like? What can I give you to remind you of us every day of your life?"

Kinga couldn't think of a thing. Her father already had taken care of everything she might need, even finding maids-in-waiting to accompany her on her journey and stay with her in Poland.

But one evening when the whole family was eating the evening meal, her eyes came to rest on the small dishes of pure white crystals that were mined in Marmorusz. "Salt is something we always use," she thought. "I wonder if they have salt in Poland!" She thought about the salt springs from which they obtained the clear, white crystals.

The next time King Bela went to visit the salt mine, Kinga asked to go along. At the mine, she watched workman bring up barrels of brine; salt crystals would remain after the water had evaporated.

"Please, Father," she said. "I would like to take salt to Poland!" And she took off her small gold ring, with a stone, red as the fine Hungarian wines and threw it down the shaft, as a sign of taking possession.

King Bela looked at the her with surprise. Why take a common thing like salt, he wondered. But he was only to happy to grant her wish.

"Of course, I can't take the whole mine, Father," she laughed. "But I'll take as many sackfuls of our white salt as possible!"

When it was time for the journey to begin, carts were loaded with jewels and gold and silver and with bags of Hungarian salt! They traveled for many days, through forests and the Carpathian mountain passes and in the autumn they arrived in Krakow.

Such a wedding! The castle and cathedral rang out with song and laughter, with music and dancing for twelve days and nights. The people came from far and near to see their new Princess and were astonished at her beauty. She was polite and loving to all, even though she knew no one.

For four years the Prince and Princess were happy but then terrible times came upon the lands, with Tartar invasions. The land was devastated and worst of all, Prince Boleslaw was dead. Kinga shared her grief with the rest of the poor people and spent much of her time traveling among the poor, providing what help she could.

One day she came to Bochnia, a place known for salty brine-water.

"Drill a well here." she told the townspeople. "Perhaps we will find salt such as in my native land." She hoped they would strike a salt spring, where they would be able to extract salt as they did in Hungary. It would help lift the spirits of the destitute people, with a little flavoring for their meager diet.

She watched as the workers dug deep into the earthy clay.

But they came across no brine. Instead, they found rock-salt. They brought a large chunk of rock-salt to her feet. It glittered like a piece of ice.

The worker smashed the block to bits with one blow of his hammer. Among the bits and pieces lay a small gold ring, with a stone red as Hungarian wine!

"That's my ring," the astonished Kinga cried. "But how can that be?" Hadn't she thrown the ring down the salt shaft in Marmorusz many years ago? Was this King Bela's present to his young daughter? Kinga wondered about it and decided that in some strange way, her father had indeed given her a gift of salt to share with her new countrymen.

"Yes," she told the townspeople, "we will drill a shaft here and mine for crystals of salt, this seasoning of foods, that gives zest to life."

The mine, begun in 1253, is called Wieliczka and became the largest in Poland.

EIGHT MILES SOUTH-EAST OF KRAKOW, *the largest and oldest salt mine in Poland produces 700 tons of salt a day. Salt deposits were formed 20 million years ago when the land was covered by the warm waters of the Miocene Sea.*

Through an evaporation process, salt was being produced by 3500 B. C. Salt crystals are often embedded with coral, fossilized dates, pine cones or nuts.

The mine goes down into the earth one and one-half miles and spreads out under the town. Today, twenty worked-out chambers hold full-sized figures, carved from the salt crystal. Queen Kinga's Chapel is the largest, 180 feel long and forty feet high. (During the war, Germans manufactured aircraft parts in the huge hall)

A chapel stands at one end of the hall and scenes decorate the side walls; one of them depicts the legend of Kinga finding her ring in the first lumps of rock-salt taken from the mine.

Over 7,000 people a day travel into the depths of the earth to marvel at it all.

Polish Folk Legends

Florence Waszkelewicz Clowes

OLD FALKA AND THE SLEEPING GIANTS

In the valley of Koscielisko, on the way to the Smytnia meadow, is a high peak called Pisana. People tell different stories about it but Falka's tale is the best of all.

One day a stranger came to Falka's forge and asked him if he could make golden horseshoes. "Why not? After all, I'm a blacksmith!" And so Falka set to work, making many horseshoes and nails for him. Then the stranger put everything in a sack and asked Falka to follow him.

As they approached the Pisana peak, he turned and said, "Don't be afraid. Just walk as quietly as possible and don't say a word!"

Falka followed, along a mountain grove and into a hole in the side of the hill. They walked and walked until they reached the center of the cave. Around were soldiers with beards down to their belts. Falka whispered, "Who are they?"

"They are the knights of King Boleslaw, waiting to be called to defend Poland. The horses must be kept shod and ready to serve their masters."

The knights were dressed in battle armor, with their swords and lances in their hands. The horses, too, had breastplates and frontal pieces and stood motionless, with their riders.

Soon the blacksmith was busy at work, fitting the horseshoes to the hooves and hammering in the nails. Time stood still as Falka quietly worked on the horses. The stranger stood by, saying nothing.

At last all were finished and Falka looked at the man.

He took some gold shavings from the floor and asked Falka to fill his sack with them. "While you're at it, clean up the horse droppings, too."

41

Falka looked cross and grumbled to himself. "So this is the pay I get for all that work. Some small gold shavings and big horse droppings!"

His sack was full, the floor cleaned up and the stranger motioned the way out of the cave.

They walked silently down the mountain path, until they came to the meadows. "You can find your way now," the stranger said. "You did an excellent job. and I hope to find you next year." With that, he vanished.

Falka sat down by the roadside for a rest, for the sack had been heavy to carry. "There's no need for me to carry all those horse droppings any farther," he thought and he spilled the contents on the ground, being careful to keep the gold shavings.

When he arrived home, his wife was amazed.

"Where have you been for three days?"

"I didn't know where the time had flown, it seemed just a short while," he exclaimed. "And look what I've got—a few gold shavings!" He shook his bag out on the table and the shavings dropped out. And then—clunk, clunk! Two huge gold nuggets rolled out.

"Well, I'll be!" declared Falka. "Those were the horse droppings I picked up!'' And then he settled down to tell his wife of the strange adventure. When they hurried back to the meadow, the horse droppings were nowhere in sight.

"I won't be so dumb next time!"

And sure enough, the stranger came again the following year and asked him to make some golden horseshoes and follow him to the secret mountain cave. Falka was only too happy to do so and gathered the horseshoes, nails, his tools and a very large sack and followed the stranger.

Again, time seemed to stand still as Falka shod horse after horse and looked at the horse droppings and golden shavings on the floor. When he was almost finished, the stranger again asked him to clean up the floor. Falka swept the floor clean with his hands, until suddenly he caught a sliver in his finger. "Psiakrew!" he cried.

"What? Did you call?" some of the knights near him began to waken.

But the stranger said, "No one called. Not yet. Sleep on!" He gave Falka a dirty look and they hurried out of the cave.

When Falka arrived home that evening, he was too excited to be tired. "Look," he cried to his wife. "Look at the full bag I have this time!" And he turned the bag out on the floor. Horse droppings and gold shavings rolled out. A large amount of horse droppings, for that was what Falka gathered most of all! The gold shavings looked tiny in that large pile.

He had been punished for breaking the silence and was never called back to the cave again.

Psiakrew—literally 'dog's blood'. A curse word.

MANY, MANY YEARS AFTER THIS STORY TOOK PLACE, *the King of Poland, seeing that the country was in great trouble, decided to call King Boleslaw's Sleeping Knights to the rescue. He called on his wise men for advice; no one knew where the cave was.*

An old prophetess declared that three brothers—to each of whom she gave a portion of a flute—must travel over seven mountains and seven rivers until they came to a certain peak in the Carpathians. There they must put the pieces together and blow. In response, King Boleslaw and his armored knights would waken from their sleep and would come forth once more to conquer and restore the land.

The brothers, representing Aristocracy, Bourgeois and Peasantry, traveled the land, but when they came to the peak, they could not agree on who should blow the flute. Each thought himself entitled to that honor.

The knights slept on, for no sound was ever heard!

TALES OF A SLEEPING ARMY *waiting to be called back from the dead at the moment of supreme need are popular and numerous. Poland has King Boleslaw, Spain has Boabdil, Germany has Barbarossa, to mention a few.*

Over fifty variants are listed in the Catalog of Polish Folktales by Julian Krzyzanowski. The celebrated legend of the Returning Hero is well known in Europe and England.

LECA BOCIANY

"Dziadzio, Dziadzio, the storks are coming!" Tadek called, as he ran to the garden where his grandfather was working.

The old man looked up at the sky, now filled with hundreds of storks, their huge wings blocking out the sun. "Ah! When the first storks you see are flying, you will have a happy and good year! But I knew they would soon be here."

"How did you know?"

Grandfather sat down on the bench. "It's spring, isn't it? Every year the storks leave their home in Africa and fly north to visit us! And the other day I saw some advance scouts out in the fields. They always travel ahead of the flock, checking things out."

"Oh, our Bocieniu will be happy to see them!" said Tadek. He thought about their pet stork and how Grandpa and he had mended its broken wing and taken care of it when the rest of the storks had flown south last fall.

All winter long it followed Tadek around and on the coldest winter nights, Babcia let the stork sleep in the cottage instead of the barn. Now there would be other storks around.

"Will Bocieniu find a mate this summer?"

"No, I'm afraid not." Grandfather shook his head sadly.

"But why not, Dziadzio? He's fully grown by now and can fly, too."

"Ah, little one, storks are very wise. Once a stork has become a pet, the other storks will have nothing to do with him. They think he has become too much like humans. And rightly so. Don't we feed him? He doesn't know how to search for food, or survive in the wilds. He hasn't been taught by his parents the things a bird should know. It seems cruel, no? But storks are very loving and caring with their young. Remember when the neighbor's barn burned down, the one with the stork nest on top?"

"Oh, yes. I remember the awful cries of the young birds, because they couldn't fly yet and were caught in the nest."

"And do you remember how the parents tried to get them out? And when they couldn't, what happened? They stayed right there with their young and perished right along with them!"

Tadek laid on the grass and buried his head in the tall blades. He didn't like to think of that awful day. He could still hear the clacking of the young birds. Suddenly he sat up. It wasn't his imagination. The flock of storks had landed in the fields and were strutting around, searching for food.

"Look," Dziadzio coaxed the grandson. "See how they eat the bugs and mice in the fields? They always bring us good luck. Don't feel sad! You know they come to visit us every summer!

"Soon they will be looking for a place to build their nest and the same storks that were here last year will come to us again. The young storks that are selecting a mate will look for the tallest place they can find to build a nest—a treetop, a chimney or the wagon wheel on top of the barn. They will lay some eggs, hatch some chicks and raise a family before they leave in the fall.

"My grandfather would tell me the tale about God punishing the storks but I don't think that God punished those beautiful birds!"

"What was that, Dziadzio? Tell me!"

"Well, my Dziadzio said long ago storks had feathers that were magnificent, in the most dazzling colors, better than any other bird. But the storks became conceited and arrogant with their beautiful coats.

"When the time of the Big Flood came, Noah urged all the animals, birds and beasts to enter his Ark. Everyone was sad to leave his home but they were grateful to Noah for saving them. Everyone except the storks, that is! They weren't grateful to

Noah, they weren't sad to leave their home! God punished them by taking away their beautifully colored feathers and leaving them with a white coat, their wings a mournful black.

"After the flood, the other creatures were happy to be alive and have new homes but the storks longed for their beautiful plumage and their former homes—Poland and Africa. And when they are in one place, they longed to be at the other, eternally wandering back and forth over the continents!"

"Oh, Dziadzio, I don't think the storks are conceited! Look how our Bocieniu follows me around and clucks when we feed him!"

"I like to think of the storks as wise and caring birds," said Dziadzio. "They are very intelligent, you know. In the fall, when it is time for them to travel south again, they will hold a *Sejm* in the empty fields. It is like a great convention, every stork will walk around clucking, trying to convince the other storks of its superiority. Soon, they will choose a leader and this *Ciemiezca*, the King Stork, will set a date for their departure.

"He will walk through the group and select those that are not strong enough to make the trip. They won't be allowed to travel, like our Bocieniu. Most of the birds that are left become pampered pets for the rest of their lives.

"The flock will follow the *Ciemiezca* south, down around the shores of the Mediterranean to Africa and Asia, where they stay for the winter. They have been doing this for thousands of years, maybe even before Noah and the flood!"

A loud clucking noise drowned out grandfather's talk. At the tip of the barn roof, in the old wagon wheel, a pair of storks began filling it with bits of straw, making a fresh nest for the summer!

The Sejm is the Polish parliament.

DUE TO THEIR CARE AND CONCERN FOR THEIR YOUNG, *storks are depicted as delivering babies. One of the traditional songs of the Polish wedding feast supports this, with the bride singing:*

"When I was a young girl,
I was told storks brought babies.
Now I am told, if I don't make love
The stork won't bring the baby!''

Storks migrate between Africa and Europe each year, flying the same route and avoiding large bodies of water, like the Mediterranean Sea. In the long journey, they follow the thermal waves across Africa and Europe. This enables them to take advantage of air currents and sometimes coast across the skies, much as our airplanes do today.

Polish Folk Legends

SCOLNUS

Long, long ago there lived a brave sailor-knight, who was bound to the service of the Danish King Christian. He loved the sea and spent many days sailing the Baltic with his fellow sailors. King Christian gave him many goods to deliver to distant shores and towns along the coast.

But Jan Scolnus was an adventurous man. He wanted to learn more about the sea and the lands beyond. He went to the King. "I want to sail west and discover the lands of which others speak." He begged the king for permission to start on an expedition and to finance the trip.

The King thought of the glory it would bring but first he met with his councilors. "It would bring great prestige if the Pole were to find new lands," said one.

"Our trade would increase and we would be masters of the seas," said another. But there were two who secretly hated and feared Scolnus.

"Don't believe him, your Highness. There are no lands across the sea," the monk, Gundolf, argued.

Finally the King declared, "I believe in him and I will finance the expedition."

His messenger carried the news to Scolnus. "The King has granted permission for your journey, Scolnus. He has assigned two witnesses to travel with you and make a report."

The monk, Gundolf and Hugo Roth, the enemies of Scolnus were to travel with him!

Scolnus spent many weeks outfitting his ship, the Swan and recruiting men. He had a following of men but for this long trip they would need many more. At last everything was in order and the Swan set sail for the unknown. Gundolf and Roth kept a close watch on their captain.

After sailing for weeks, a huge iceberg suddenly loomed up in front of the ship. The crew panicked and Scolnus' enemies seized the opportunity to encourage a mutiny.

A fight broke out. "Let's return, let's sail back home," the sailors cried. But there were others that were faithful to Scolnus and they were able to persuade the sailors to return to their oars and obey Scolnus. Roth was thrown overboard for encouraging the mutiny!

For three months—three months of sailing over an uncharted sea—the Swan continued West. And then land was sighted!

"Hurray, hurray!" shouted the men and they forgot their days of weariness. They had reached the land now called Labrador!

The icy land didn't interest them and after planting the Danish flag on the soil, Scolnus and his crew set sail for home. He had discovered the mysterious land of the West!

The monk, Gundolf, wrote down his observations but he was never able to make his report to King Christian, for he died on board the Swan, before reaching Denmark.

And so it was that a Pole, in the fifteenth Century, discovered the North American continent.

THE CHRONICLE OF KORNELIUS WYTFIELD, *in the year 1599, reads: "Jan Scolnus, Pole (of Kolno, near Gdansk), in the year 1476, sailed along the coast of Norway, Greenland and Frisland. He entered the North Sea and reached the lands of Larradoris and Estolandia, which were protected by an icy climate and a rough sea."*

LITTLE HALINA OF SANDOMIERZ

Halina covered her ears with her hands. The Tartars were attacking again! The walls of Sandomierz protected her and the townspeople from the arrows and spears of the invaders but the clashing armor, the cries of the men and horses echoed over the sandy plain and drifted over the high walls and down into the Vistula.

Almost everyone hid in their cellars during such raids. Many cellars were connected with long tunnels, which led from one part of the town to another. Halina thought there were as many alleys under the town as there were on top of the ground.

Her father, the bailiff, had a large house with three systems of cellars underneath. There was one trap door in the house, one in the courtyard and one in the corridor. One of the cellars was a large room, with a curved ceiling like a church. Halina's father had urged his daughter to stay near one of the trap doors. He wanted his only child to be safe, while he led a group of men through the town gate to battle the Tartars.

But Halina climbed up the tower steps instead and squeezed into one of the vacant narrow watchtower windows. She covered her ears as the Tartars thundered down, with their horses breathing hard, the men's spears and armor shining in the sun. She watched the attack on the small band of valiant Poles. She watched them fight and get struck down one by one. She thought she saw her father. And then he was struck down!

For a long time she sat at the window, seeing nothing. First her mother—and now her father—was dead. She wondered why there had to be so much fighting, why the Tartars kept attacking the town. Trade routes from all directions came to Sandomierz. People from the Baltic to the Black Sea met here to trade spices, teas, oriental rugs, salt, amber and grain! Why did the Tartars want to spoil it all?

When she looked out the window again, it had grown dark. Huge campfires on the plain warmed the weary wounded warriors. Suddenly, she jumped up and ran down the steps to the marketplace—she had a plan.

Halina burst in on the Elder's meeting; men grieving over the loss of their leader and many good friends. Feeling there were not enough men left to fight another day, they were planning to surrender.

"Wait!" Halina stopped the talk.

At any other time she would have been sent scurrying out of the room but tonight was different. The men were tired, discouraged and defeated.

"I have a plan. Let me try something tonight. If it doesn't work, you can surrender in the morning."

The men had decided to wait until morning anyway, so they listened to her. They thought the plan was foolish and had little chance of succeeding but it gave them a faint flicker of hope. So they agreed and Halina ran off.

The guard opened the gate for her and she slipped out into the darkness. She buried her hands deep in her apron pockets to keep them from shaking and her body was tingling all over as she headed for the light of the campfires.

Halfway there she was lifted up in the air by a soldier on horseback. "What have we here?" he shouted to his companions. He rode toward the group, carrying Halina like a sack of potatoes, on one arm.

Dropped into the center of the band, she looked at the bloody, exhausted men. They didn't look so fearsome anymore and it gave her new courage. Their leader sat on a carpet, legs crossed, calmly smoking.

"Well, is this all that's left of Sandomierz?" he laughed.

"Don't talk to me of Sandomierz! They are a bunch of lazy, ignorant people. They are cowards and I am ashamed of them!"

The men laughed at the spunky little girl. Before they could wonder how she had gotten there, she continued. "I can show you a way to the center of the town and an easy victory!"

"Really!"

"I will lead you into the town, if you will spare my life and give me two pigeons!"

Pigeons, thought the leader. This girl is simple-minded!

"I love pigeons! They are free to come and go from the towers to the trees, to the hills and valleys. I want to be free like them!"

"Ho, a pigeon you will be! What is this great plan you have to offer?"

She told them of an underground tunnel into the town. The entrance, hidden in the slope of the land, lay outside the town walls. She, herself, would lead the way, through a maze of tunnels to the center of the town! All for two pigeons and freedom!

The leader thought for a long time. The very center of town, without bloodshed! From that vantage point, his tired men could make an easy conquest.

"Give the girl her pigeons!" he called. "Small price—pigeons or her head!"

Just before daybreak Halina lead the band of Tartars to the *Piszczele*, a sunken section of ground near the wall that held an entrance to a secret tunnel. She showed the invaders where to uncover the trap door and led them into the tunnel, a small lantern in one hand and two pigeons in a sack in the other. The men followed.

From a distance, a small group of townspeople stood ready, hidden in the predawn darkness. When they though the Tartars were far enough into the tunnel, they closed the opening with the stones and heaped dirt all around. Then they returned to the marketplace, awaiting the next part of their plan.

Halina knew where she would lead them. Not to the center of the town but to one of the cellars long abandoned as being unsafe. As she entered the room, she stumbled, dropping the sack with the pigeons and the lantern crashed on the floor, broken.

Freed, the pigeons quickly worked their way though cracks and crevices in the dirt walls and fluttered back to fresh air and freedom.

The townspeople watched as the birds flew to the rooftops in the early morning sunlight. This was their signal to seal off all entrances to the cellars. Desperately they waited, watching to see if Halina would escape also. But no, she, too, was trapped with the invaders!

Brave and unafraid, she had led the Tartars to their doom and sacrificed her own life for the lives of the townspeople of Sandomierz!

SANDOMIERZ, LIKE AN ICEBERG, *goes much deeper underground than it rises above ground. The system of underground corridors is much more complicated than the town's street system. In its early days, the underground part was used as storerooms for goods and also as a hiding place from Tartar attacks, with traps set for invaders. A 17th Century house, No. 31, has three systems of cellars, each with a separate entrance.*

Archeologists have found many records that identify Sandomierz as one of the early neolithic settlements. Located near the fork of the Vistula and San rivers, the water and fertile flat plains resulted in the site becoming an important town. It grew in importance when a trade route was developed by the Indo-European people (c 7000-4000 B.C.) following the steppe roads between the marshes of Prypec and the Carpathian Mountains.

Polish Folk Legends

THE AGES OF MAN

There are all kinds of people made of flesh and blood—hey! When the Lord God created animals, he called the lion and said, "You will rule over the animals, while I rule over man."

What happened then? It so happened that an ox, donkey, calf and dog got together and decided to oust the lion from power, so they could rule themselves—hey!

They planned together. The calf bleated pitifully as if it were hungry and the ox walked behind and explained why it was bleating—for the calf was a very stupid animal. They explained that the lion didn't give them anything to eat and only beat them. The donkey raised and lowered his ears to show that the lion was always at odds with him, too.

It so happened that the lion found out what was going on and called everyone to his den. "You know—you are all acting very stupidly. Who put you up to this?" They all pleaded innocent and no one would confess to any part of it.

"The devil must have gotten into you since you acted so stupidly—hey! Do you think it's fun to rule. The Lord commanded me and I must obey. Since you have sinned, you must take your medicine. I'll mete out your punishment right away."

But the lion didn't want to punish them all by himself because it didn't pay to mess around with them. He therefore ordered the ox to eat the dog and the donkey to eat the ox and the calf to eat the donkey.

But the calf had trouble eating the donkey because its bones were hard. He gnawed and gnawed and broke all his teeth but he finally ate the donkey except for its head. The lion finally ate the calf, after all the other animals had been eaten but was afraid to eat the head because it was—pardon the expression—

damn stupid. Then he buried the heads and skins and leftover bones in the ground and so they rotted.

Finally the Lord God decided to create man. He took some mud and formed man. But alas, he created him on the very spot where those stupid animals were buried—hey!

For that reason, man—even the wisest farmer—comes from those beasts. When he is young he is stupid as a calf. When he grows up he chases around like a dog and won't settle down. When he marries he works like an ox and when old age catches up with him, he become stubborn like a donkey—hey!

But only men are like that, for women were created later—hey!

THE HIGHLANDERS HAD THEIR OWN THEORY *of the evolution and development of man long before Darwin came on the scene. This tale was collected in Zakopane by A. Stopka in 1894 and published by Julian Krzyanowski in 1897, in his Sabata. Krzyanowski is perhaps the most widely known folklorist in Poland.*

PATRON SAINT OF POLAND

Long, long ago, when Poland was still a young country, there was a bishop who traveled through the countries of Europe, preaching the word of God. Adalbert was the Bishop of Prague and one day Emperor Otto III sent him to convert the wild and cruel Prussians to Christianity. He traveled first to Poland to visit Boles the Brave, Prince of Poland at Gniezno.

Emperor Otto and Boleslaw were friends and Boleslaw treated the bishop kindly. He ordered his soldiers to escort the bishop and the few monks with him to the Prussian border. The small group fearlessly continued on their way into Prussian land, searching for its people.

First, they came across a small hut in a small clearing near the road. An old woman came out of the hut to greet the strangers and kindly offered them a drink. Adalbert was surprised to find an old women living alone in the woods and alone in this fearful land.

"Don't the Prussians harm you? Aren't you afraid to live out here by yourself?" he asked.

"Ach," she laughed. "The Prussians know I am so poor, I have nothing to give them. Sometimes they even leave me one of the animals they kill on their hunts. But usually they just leave me alone," she explained.

After a rest, Adalbert and his monks continued on their journey. As they left, Adalbert gave the old women a gold coin for her kindness.

Following the paths that wandered through the forest, they soon came upon a small village of the Prussians. They began talking with the people, telling them about God and preaching the Gospels. The Prussians listened but soon chased the group out of the village, throwing stones at them. Fearlessly, Adalbert continued into the wilds of the land, stopping at each village they found, preaching the word of God. But the Prussians weren't willing to change their pagan ways—they had other gods they worshiped.

At one village, the Prussians got very angry and began attacking the group with clubs and hatchets. They fell on Adalbert, who wore a large cross and tearing it off, beat him to death. The monks tried to protect him but were beaten themselves. Finally, they fled for their lives.

When Boleslaw heard Adalbert had been murdered, he sent a group of ambassadors to claim his body. He sent them with bags of gold and jewels, for he knew the Prussians would not agree to the request without a reward.

The Prussians did demand a ransom—the weight of the bishop's body in gold!

Two large baskets were placed on each end of a long pole, which was balanced on a large log. They placed Adalbert's body in one basket. The bags of gold the ambassadors had brought were placed in the other. The baskets didn't move—it wasn't enough! Desperately, they took off their jewels and gold rings—anything they had with them that was valuable—and tossed it into the basket. Still it didn't move. The Prussians stood boldly, unwilling to give up the bishop until they received its weight in gold.

Suddenly, the little old woman, who had given them refreshments earlier in their journey, appeared. When she saw what had happened, she was very sad. She took the gold coin from her pocket and tossed it into the basket.

The Prussians laughed at the woman for giving away the coin, for they knew how poor she was. But they stopped laughing when the baskets began to move!

Slowly, the basket with the gold began to sink to the ground, until the two baskets balanced exactly on the log. They stayed quite still, in mid-air—the body of Adalbert and its weight in gold.

And so the Prussians gave up Adalbert's body and it was carried back to Gniezno. Boleslaw had the martyr laid to rest in the cathedral of Gniezno and he was soon declared the patron saint of Poland. It all happened in the year 977, a long, long time ago!

BISHOP ADALBERT *(Wojciech) of Prague was none too successful in his own dioceses and was sent to Rome, Hungary and Poland to preach the word of God. He was welcomed by the people everywhere else and was considered to be one of the first missionaries to Poland.*

In 977, he was sent by Emperor Otto III to convert the pagan Prussians. He first stopped at Gniezno and visited with Boleslaw, who had earlier converted to Christianity. The trip into the wilds of Prussia lasted ten days and as he and his monks were returning to Poland, he was murdered.

Boleslaw paid a ransom for Adalbert's body equal to its weight in gold and had it brought back to Gniezno, the capital at that time. There, it was laid to rest in a church built twenty years earlier. At a time when Christianity played an important part in the political development of the country, Adalbert was canonized and Poland had its first patron saint.

Otto traveled to Gniezno to pay his respects to the martyr and strengthen the idea of a universal empire of Christians. He was given one of St. Adalbert's arms to take back to Germany.

The cathedral was destroyed in 1018, 1025 and again in 1038 by Bretuslaus of Bohemia, who carried off part of the relics of Saint Adalbert to Prague.

In 1170, magnificent bronze doors with twelve bas-reliefs were constructed. They depict the life of Saint Adalbert, (Sw. Wojciech.) Today, they are part of the post-World War II reconstructed Gniezno Cathedral.

In the center of the main nave is a cartofarge of Saint Adalbert, on top of a silver coffin which contains a 13th-Century casket reliquary with the remains of the first patron saint of Poland.

THE JEALOUS BROTHER

Once there was a great fire in the Old Town of Krakow. All the ancient buildings had been attacked and destroyed by invading tribes. Everything lay in ruins—the Cathedral, the Town Hall, the Cloth Hall—everything! But soon the townspeople began to rebuild their town. The king, of course, decided that Wawel Castle and Cathedral must be rebuilt first and so it was. All the artisans, the masons, the woodworkers were busy rebuilding for many years. When the work was completed, the knights and couriers were able to worship together with the king and the bishop but the burghers and craftsmen and the townspeople still didn't have any place to worship.

They began to grumble. "Our Lady's Church will never get rebuilt!" they thought. And so the townspeople decided to build it themselves and not wait for the tax money. Many wealthy merchants donated money and many citizens, too.

Plans were drawn up for the Gothic cathedral. Red bricks, stones and lumber were purchased and transported down the Vistula. Two brothers, the best masons in town, were hired to do the work.

They began their work eagerly and with pride. All the townspeople would see what wonderful work they were able to do and no doubt they would receive many offers of work in the future. And so they worked carefully and as quickly as possible. For many months they worked on the main body of the church and then began work on the two towers. The brothers decided to have a race to see who would be the first to complete his tower.

As time went on it became apparent that one tower was growing much faster than the other and the slower of the two brothers became worried.

"How is it that you are able to build your tower so fast?" has asked. "Are the laborers bringing you bigger bricks?"

"No," laughed the quick one. "I am working faster than you and will finish first! Too bad you aren't as quick and nimble as I," he teased.

With that the slower brother drew his knife. "I'll show you how nimble and quick I am!" and he sprang forward with his knife, killing his brother instantly.

When he realized what he had done, he dropped his knife and fled to the Vistula, where he drowned in his sorrow.

For this reason, one of the towers is taller than the other. The townspeople lost their desire to complete the tower and in their sorrow, hung the knife on a chain near the gate to the Cloth Hall, so all could see the evil that had been done.

Many years went by before the towers were completed, with a globe and crown placed on the steeple of the taller one. And even today, Krakowianians will tell you this story of the two brothers!

THE CHURCH OF THE BLESSED MARY *(Mariacki) is one of the most beautiful landmarks in Krakow. It is the chief parish for the city and contains the most beautiful medieval altar in Europe.*

First built in 1226, it was destroyed in a devastating fire that destroyed the majority of buildings in the Old Town. The church was rebuilt with monies collected from wealthy merchants in 1418 but the towers weren't finished until much later. The taller of the two was finished in 1478 and the lower tower completed in 1573.

Many restoration projects were undertaken during the First Secretary Edward Gierak's regime, one being restoration of the two steeples of the Mariacki.

The golden globe which rests on the taller of the two was removed for cleaning and inspection. Many documents were found inside, describing previous restoration works in 1418, 1545 and 1562. Other items included coins from the reign of Stanislaus Augustus, medals from the 1863 National Uprising, a 1836 map of Krakow and a copy of the Krakow Gazette, dated July 22, 1843.

Wit Stwosz, a talented Polish artist from Nuremberg, was contracted to carve the altar in 1477. The large polychrome triptych, carved in linden wood, represents scenes in the life of the Virgin Mary. It took him twelve years to complete the work.

During World War II, the Poles dismantled the altar and prepared to ship it to Sweden for safekeeping. The Germans, however, confiscated it instead and sent it to Nuremberg, where it was hidden in a cellar sixty feet underground. It was found by the United States Army in 1946 and returned to Krakow where it was restored to its original place.

The Church of the Blessed Virgin Mary is still a most beautiful building and perhaps best known for its story of' 'The Broken Note.'' But that is another story!

SUWALKI TREASURES

Long, long ago some monks lived in the deep forests of the Suwalki region, in northeast Poland. It was a beautiful place, with lakes and streams and the woods were full of mushrooms and blackberries. The monks spent their time praying—that is, when they weren't eating.

The Superior of Camedolite monastery liked nothing better than a fine meal and fortunately, he had a good cook. Barnaba was an expert at cooking and he would turn out the most tasty dishes day after day.

But as the years went by it became harder and harder to please the Superior. One day, in desperation, Barnaba paced about the terraces, trying to think up something different for his superior. He knew he would be severely reprimanded if he didn't satisfy his boss. Absentmindedly he gazed at the nearby Lake Jodel.

He laughed out loud, thinking of the story of Ortus, the God of the Lithuanian lakes. The ancient Luthuanians, Jaacwingi, told a legend about the lake and their God. Ortus, disguised as a dog, protected the lake and its treasures.

On the night of a full moon, a floating chest of treasure could be seen in the lake. The chest sparkled in the moonlight, full of silver and gold. Anyone who tried to reach the treasure was stopped by the growling God-dog and the treasure disappeared into the depths of the lake.

"Treasure indeed!" Barnaba laughed. "A treasure would be to catch a lavaret from the lake!" He was thinking of the tasty fish found in Italian lakes. "Then I would surely please the Superior!" He flung a stone skimming across the lake's waters with all his might. "Go to the devil," he cried.

Instantly he looked about sheepishly, ashamed of his outburst. But there was no one around and he settled down for a nap.

He awoke to a swooshing sound. There before him stood a stranger in strange clothing, with a cajoling smile on his lips. He pulled a paper out of his pocket and began to talk to Barnaba in a soothing voice.

"Before the bells toll of the martins, I'll be back with a basket full of lavarets for you! Won't that be nice for a change? And all you have to do for the favor is give me your soul!"

Half asleep, Barnaba signed the paper placed before him.

The swooshing sound of the disappearing devil brought him to his senses, however. "Mother of God, what have I done," he cried as he wondered what made him do such a foolish thing, which doomed him to damnation.

Quickly he hurried to the Superior and confessed his sin. Together they prayed and thought and thought and prayed. Finally they agreed, there was no other way but to deceive the devil. Trembling with fear and excitement, they set their plan and waited in readiness in the bell tower.

Well before midnight they could hear a shrill whiz and noise in the distance—the devil was approaching with fish in his arms. Quickly the monks began pulling at the ropes of the bells. The silvery sound of the bells rang out over the countryside and pierced the ears of the flying devil.

Thinking he had missed the midnight deadline he became furious. He was late and had lost his power over Barnaba! He flung the lavaret into the lake and disappeared in a wisp of black cloud.

From that time on, the monks enjoyed many tasty meals of lavaret.

LAVARET, (WHITEFISH) ARE USUALLY *found in Central Europe. The Suwalki lakes provide carp, trout, eel and salmon. This district has been preserved in its natural surroundings.*

The wealth of timber provides lumber for furniture industries which developed in the 1960s but the charms of nature continue to lure tourists into the area.

The "treasure" of the lake, as many of Poland's treasures, lies deep in the ground. In 1962, rich poly-metallic deposits were discovered in the region. The deposits, high in iron content, also contain vanadium, nickel, cobalt and titanium. Could it be some of the elements were reflected in the waters of Lake Jodel?

JERZY, A KNIGHT IN SHINING ARMOR

Once upon a time, there was a monster that lived in a small lake near a small town. Every day he would rise out of the waters of the lake and roar with hunger. He would eat anyone and anything that happened to be nearby.

At times, finding nothing to eat on the shores of the lake, he would crawl to the town. The townspeople tried to fight him off but it was impossible. His every breath was poison to one and all.

"What should we do?" they cried. "Everyone will be eaten alive!"

And so it was decided to feed the monster-dragon with sheep. Each day, two sheep were left on the lakeshore, where the dragon would satisfy his hunger.

Well, before long all the sheep in the town were gone, even all the animals in the field outside the town. The townspeople held a meeting. In desperation, they agreed to offer themselves! Each day a person would be chosen for the sacrifice. No family was spared.

One day the lot fell to the Princess. Horror-stricken, the king offered half his gold, half his silver, half his kingdom, in his desire to save his daughter.

"Oh, no," cried the townspeople. "Why should we suffer and not you?" All the king could obtain was a seven day delay of the sacrifice.

The days flew by quickly and the king had no choice but to abide by the decisions of the townspeople. His dressed his daughter in the finest royal clothes and led her to the edge of the lake, where he left her, weeping.

81

Now there happened to be a knight riding by. "Why are you crying?" he asked.

"Good soldier, mount your horse and ride away as fast as you can. If you don't, you will die with me!"

But Jerzy said, "Don't worry about me! Why are you crying and why are the townspeople and the king mourning on the hillside?"

"Oh," she wailed, "there's a monster in this lake! A monster-dragon so wicked it eats everything in sight. We have sacrificed all our animals and now we offer ourselves so the other townspeople may remain safe for a while longer. Many brave men have tried to slay the dragon but have only lost their own lives! Go away, or you will be next!"

At that moment, the dragon rose out of the water and the young princess screamed. "Go away, go away while you still can!"

But Jerzy made the sign of the cross and, asking God to protect him, headed toward the lake. When the dragon crawled on shore, Jerzy could see what a terrible monster he really was. Bravely he attacked with his swift sword. With one blow, he knocked the dragon unconscious!

With his foot on the dragon's head, he called to the Princess, "Quick, give me your belt!" He looped his belt tightly around the dragon's neck and when the stunned dragon awoke, he submitted to Jerzy, who led him like a tame dog toward the town.

The townspeople fled in fear but Jerzy called, "There's no need to be afraid any longer! The Lord sent me to save you from this evil dragon!"

When they heard this, the king and all his people, twenty-thousand men, not counting women and children, were baptized! Then Jerzy cut off the head of the frightful monster. For the rest of his days he was honored as a chivalrous knight, a solder-saint who faithfully served the Lord.

THE NATIONAL MUSEUM IN GDANSK, *situated in a former Franciscan monastery, holds valuable works of art from Medieval times to the present. The sculpture of Sw. Jerzy (St. George) slaying the dragon is ascribed to Hans Brandt (1485c). Carved in linden wood, it is one of the finest examples of the cultivation of knightly qualities. Created during the Gothic period at a time when patron saints were assigned to different trades, St. George, in his suit of armor and coat of mail became the patron saint of knights.*

The crusades further enhanced his image and he became the patron saint of England, Argon and Portugal.

The port town of Gdansk, a part of the important trade routes from the Baltic to the Black Sea, became a part of world history and developed world legacies.

The beginnings of this tale are lost in antiquity but dragon-slaying myths date back to the third Century B.C. in Sumerian mythology. This popular tale of ancient heathen Europe relates to the strife between the sun and the demon of darkness, or storm. When Christianity developed, St. George was identified as the sun and the dragon as the darkness.

Christianity accepts George as living in the 4th Century, A.D. He underwent great suffering in seven days, or seven weeks, of persecution and torture by Emperor Diocletian when he refused to denounce his Christian faith.

Miraculous events during this trial led to the conversion of Empress Alexandra. Diocletian was so exasperated, he ordered both the Empress and George executed.

In the middle ages, April 23 was assigned the saint's day.

It replaced the ancient pagan festival of Parilia, a festival of Love. The day of fertility of the immortal gods was transformed into a day devoted to the fertility of the fields. They are blessed by a parish priest just when the green crops are beginning to emerge from the earth. He invokes God to provide a bountiful harvest.

St. George is any Christian who is Christ's faithful soldier and servant throughout his life. Armed with a breastplate of righteousness, a shield of faith, a helmet of salvation and a sword of the Spirit, he is called to fight the dragon, the devil who poisons the streams of grace and seeks to devour the pure of heart.

THE GOLDEN CUP OF KASIMIR

Elzbieta and her brother Stefan lived in the old town of Bedzin. It was a very old town but King Kasimir the Great had recently built a beautiful new stone castle to replace the old one, a great parish church and a wall to fortify the town. Everyone felt very secure with their new buildings and for a while no invaders bothered them.

But one day news came from Sandomierz that the invading hordes of Genghis Khan were attacking villages and sweeping across the Polish plains. The knights and warriors of the town prepared for battle and rode out to meet them, hoping to save their home and families from the horrors of war. Fourteen-year old Elzbieta and her younger brother were left behind in the castle, with only the servants to care for them. From the high castle tower, Elzbieta and Stefan watched as billowing smoke from burning villages filled the sky.

It wasn't long before the Tartars were at the castle gates. The town was fortified but there was no one to protect it and soon the invaders were torching houses and shouting great war cries. The women and children ran and hid as best they could.

At the castle walls Prince Batu, leader of the forces of Emperor Ogdai, son of Genghis Khan, reined his horse. "Here lies the golden cup of Kasimir! We'll take it back to our ruler!" he shouted and the warriors began to break down the door.

Everyone in the castle was frightened and began to shudder. The servants ran and hid. Elzbieta looked about the beautiful rooms, so full of rich tapestries, inlaid wooden floors, oak furniture and gold and silver ornaments, sad to know they would soon be destroyed.

Suddenly she ran to the chapel. There on the altar stood the beautiful cup of Kasimir. Worked by silversmiths in Krakow, it sparkled with its insert of precious stones. An inscription around the rim, written in Latin, read: "Blest Be The Life That Drinks From Me." To drink from King Kasimir's cup while receiving communion—was a sign of power and many believed it gave mystical protection.

Now Prince Batu wanted the cup.

Elzbieta picked up the cup and ran to the kitchen. "Where can we hide it?" she asked the cook. Stas looked at her in wonder. Everyone else was fearful for their life, although he himself wasn't afraid. They wouldn't kill a cook, fighting men like to eat as well as anyone else. But Elzbieta so young and innocent, what would the Tartars do with her? And here she was worrying about the King's cup instead of her own life.

"Here," he cried, "hide in the soot box."

She climbed in the large box standing near the fireplace and Stas covered her with rags and sprinkled soot over her and the cup.

Batu was a fierce, ruthless man. He had heard about the golden cup and was determined to get it. When the castle doors were finally broken down, he entered the great hall and shouted. "Bring me the cup and you will not be harmed!"

No one answered. The servants were hiding in fear and the castle was still. Suddenly Stefan came running into the room, swinging a broken sword in Batu's face. The sword was almost as big as Stefan and Batu was so surprised at the attack, he didn't know what to do. He stood motionless for a minute.

In that minute Stefan ran to the balcony and jumped over it, falling into the lake below. Stas, in the kitchen, saw him fall and ran out to help him. He dragged the unconscious boy from the water and hid him in the bushes away from Batu's sight. When Stefan revived, Stas took off the boy's wet clothing and gave him some old peasant clothes to wear, so Batu wouldn't recognize him. Then he hid the boy's fine clothes.

In the distance Stas and Stefan could see the knights of Bedzin returning to the town, having regained their strength.

Stas and the boy ran to warn them. Preparing to do battle, they entered the castle but no one was there. Batu and his men had already ransacked the place, leaving behind the dead and silent shell of the building.

Stas cried out in horror and ran down to the kitchen. Trembling with fear, he wondered, had Elzbieta been found? Did they take her and the golden cup? He raised the soot box lid and saw a slight movement. "Elzbieta," he whispered anxiously.

Elzbieta stood up, shaking the rags, soot and ashes off her. She smiled and handed Stas the golden cup of Kasimir.

KASIMIR THE GREAT *spent fifty years building a chain of churches and towns across the Polish borderlands. Some say it was a penance he was given for murdering Marcin Baryczka in 1349.*

One of these towns was Bedzin where in 1358 he ordered a parish church, The Holy Trinity, to be built, along with a stone castle and town fortifications. Goldsmiths from the royal workshops in Krakow provided the beautifully decorated chalice, at the townspeople's expense, of course.

THE LIONS OF THE GDANSK TOWN HALL

The hammer of the master stone-cutter, Daniel, clattered for days on end. From under his chisel emerged the figures of councilors and saints, night watchmen and knights. But his favorite subjects to carve were lions—gentle or fierce, peacefully dozing with drooping heads, or menacing and ready to spring.

The townspeople would stop by his workshop and watch in awe. "You really are a master craftsman. The best in the Guild. Your lions seem to be alive. It's a wonder they don't roar."

Daniel nodded and kept on working. He loved his work and was pleased that others admired his statues.

But at that time, dark clouds threatened the town, for the Prussian king, Frederick, was stretching his grasping arms toward the rich port. He tried to coerce the citizens of Gdansk to submit to his care and open the gates of the coveted city.

Instead, the citizens decided that the town hall at Dlugi Targ should be decorated. It was their way of telling Frederick they wanted no part of him. And so the mayor summoned the master sculptor to the town hall and said, "Carve us our coat of arms in stone. Let it be held by two great lions of Gdansk, full of wisdom and fearsome to our enemies. The lions will forever be a reminder of the power of our city!"

Daniel bowed low. "I am honored," he said. "I will begin at once." And with that, he returned to his workshop and began to sketch a plan. "I will try to make my lions recall the old lion virtues of Gdansk."

"What are those virtues?" his apprentice asked.

"Valor and fidelity."

"And how will you do that?"

"You will see," he said. And they set to work.

Months passed and Daniel and his apprentices worked long hours. The coat of arms was made to fit into the imposing entrance of the town hall. Two lions guarded a shield, which was decorated with two crosses under the crown of Kazimierz Jagiellonczyk.

At last all was ready for the unveiling and the townspeople gathered round. The mayor pulled down the cloth and all eyes looked up to the carving. "Ah," said everyone.

"Oh," said everyone, when they realized something was wrong.

"How could you make such a mistake?" cried the mayor. "The lions aren't looking at each other but towards the Golden Gate."

"It's not a mistake," Daniel calmly explained. "Don't you understand? The lions look toward the Golden Gate where the Royal road begins. Our kings come into the city on the Royal road and through the Golden Gate. Poland is our mother and protectress. Therefore, staunch and faithful, the lions watch for the return of our ruler."

A murmur went through the crowd. "May he return soon and protect us from our enemy!" sighed the townspeople.

Alas, the town was not protected and enemy boots trampled through the streets of the city. The statue of Neptune in the stone fountain sadly hung his head in shame. The chiming clocks on the towers of Gdansk sadly struck the hours of captivity.

Many years went by. Finally, one spring day, the walls of the town shook and the towers swayed. The mighty boom of cannons echoed through the streets and the enemy fled. The town hall lions raised their heads.

"It's Poland, returning!"

A tank with a white eagle in its turret appeared from under the arch. Others followed, driving into Dluga Street.

"Gdansk is ours again," called the soldiers. "We've got our

town back!"

The lions from the town hall shook their manes and roared joyfully to the accompaniment of the booming cannons and the roar of the Baltic waves splashing on the sandy coast of Poland.

THIS SLAVIC SETTLEMENT *is mentioned in recordings as early as 997. It developed into an important port city of Gdansk "at times called Danzig" By the 13ᵗʰ Century. After the defeat of the Teutonic Knights Gdansk swore alliance to the Polish crown in 1454. King Kazimierz IV Jagiellomczyk ruled from 1444-1492 and laid the foundation for the city's rights in freedoms in his life-giving Privilegia Casimiriama.*

The Artus Court of Gdansk at Dlugi Targ (Long Market), the seat of wealthy merchants, was famous for the large number of works of art, which speak of the city's recognition and gratitude for the centuries of just and protecting rule by Polish kings.

Many of the medieval works of art have been restored with great care and are now on display at the National Museum of Gdansk.

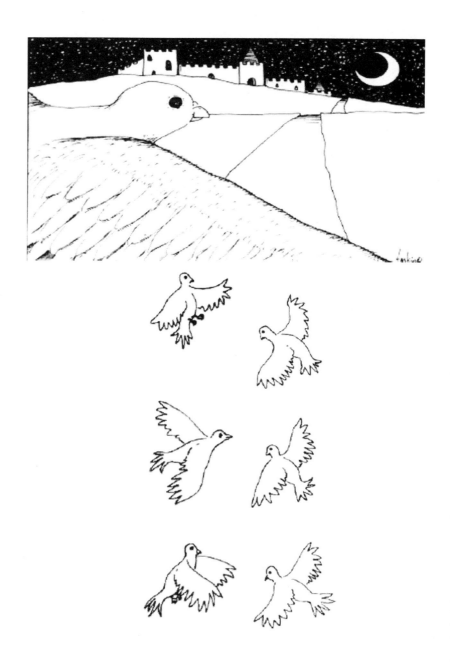

THE BEWITCHED PIGEONS

There are pigeons in Warsaw, Gdansk and Poznan but the bewitched ones are only found in Krakow. Some people know this but for those that don't, we'll tell this tale.

Once, long long ago, young Prince Henry ruled from his castle on Wawel Hill. Times were bad, enemies were continually attacking the land and there was no money to pay the armies or to protect the people. He decided to travel to visit friendly neighboring countries and establish some type of mutual protection. But there wasn't even any money for the journey.

Prince Henry called his advisors and counselors together. "Please seek out a method of sponsoring my trip," he said. "I hope to save our land by holding a summit with other friendly leaders. I will need gold for myself and my couriers for this long journey."

The advisors murmured together for a long time. Finally one of them spoke. "There is poverty in the land, the princes and nobles fight among themselves, the enemy leaves much of the land destroyed and the people suffer. There is no one to give you gold for your journey. Unless you get it by magic."

The Prince looked astonished. "Magic?"

"Yes, magic. At Zwierzyniec there lives a witch—go to her."

In the dark of the night the Prince and the knights of his court went to visit the witch. She listened to his story and nodded her grey head.

"You will get your gold, Prince Henry, if you agree to turn your entourage into birds. They will be pigeons until the day of your return."

"You want to turn my faithful friends into pigeons? Never!"

99

The Prince turned to leave.

But his faithful followers pleaded with him, "We will gladly take the form of birds, if that will help you save the country!"

And so Prince Henry agreed. Soon he was on his way, with carts loaded with gold. A fluttering flock of white pigeons descended upon the market square cooing a farewell to their Prince.

"Where did they come from?" wondered the astonished Krakowians. "What are they doing here?"

From that day on, they stayed in the market square, at times flying about the Sukiennic, St. Mary's Church or the Town tower. At other times they slowly walked about, mingling with the people, unafraid.

To this day they are waiting for their Prince to return, for he got lost somewhere on his long journey.

If you go into the Market Square and stand near the old Cloth Hall, the Sukiennic, hold out your hand. The pigeons will come at once. They will flutter over your head, or alight on your shoulder.

If you listen closely, you will hear them cooing, "Have you heard anything about our Prince? Is he coming back to free us from our spell?"

WHEN YOU ARE VISITING KRAKOW, *be sure to stop a minute and feed the pigeons. For a few zloty you can buy a bag of feed and find yourself surrounded by pigeons. They have been there for as long as anyone can remember. They even have their territories and a street named for them.*

In the center of the city you can find "Ulica Golebia" and a clerk assigned to the duty of taking care of their needs and keeping the municipal pigeon-holes tidy.

Krakow's Market Square is usually filled with people, flower stalls, cafe tables, gypsy musicians and pigeons everywhere. No trip to Poland is complete without taking in this sight and joining in to feed the pigeons.

Polish Folk Legends

THE BROKEN NOTE

The watchman climbed the narrow stairs which wound round and round, up and up to the top of the tower of St. Mary's Church. There, in a small room, he spent the night. Trumpets hung on the walls, used to sound out the hours. There was also a lantern with red glass to signal a fire at night and a red banner, to hang out the window in the daytime.

The watchmen at St. Mary's had two duties, really. They watched from the tower windows for any fires that might have started among the old wooden buildings, any riots or other danger and for any approaching troops. They would ring the bell, hang the banner or light the lantern and place it in the window facing the direction of the danger.

Their other duty was to sound out the hours, day and night, to the citizens of Krakow, by playing the sacred hymn, the *Hejnal* each hour. With their trumpet they would play the beautiful melody to the East, to the South, to the West and to the North sections of the city.

This post was very important for the safety of the townspeople and the trumpeters, or watchmen, had to take a solemn oath that they would faithfully serve the city in keeping watch and to sound the hours of the day and night.

This night wasn't like other nights, however. There had been warnings of an approaching enemy. For days people from the countryside were streaming into the city for protection. The Tartars were once again invading the land and no one was safe.

Krakow prepared for its defense. The walls were manned with citizen soldiers prepared to give their lives for the protection of the city and their families. The old castle gate opposite the Church of St. Andrew was shut and barricaded. Everyone readied themselves for the invasion.

The trumpeter took up his night post, anxiously watching and searching the skyline for signs of the invading horde. The Tartars fell upon the city in the dark of the night but the trumpeter was able to sound a warning. The townspeople fought bravely but the Tartars overwhelmed them and took the city.

They began burning and pillaging street after street until they came to the center of the city—the market place. There, in one corner of the square, stood St. Mary's Church and the trumpeter, still in one of the tall towers. He continued to sound the alarm, over and over again.

A Tartar crouched down with his bow. and pulling the string back as far as he could, let the dark shaft fly straight to its mark. It struck the trumpeter as he neared the end of his melody. He weakened for a moment, then gave one last glorious blast. The note trembled and came to a close, weak and broken. Soon the wooden church with its towers was a blazing inferno. The trumpeter perished, unable to finish the *Hejnal*.

In Poland—to this very day—the *Hejnal* is never finished. If you listen to the radio, if you are in the Market Square in Krakow, you will hear the *Hejnal* played, only to stop short on the unfinished, broken note of that trumpeter of long ago.

ONE OF THE LARGEST RAIDS *of the Tartar clans from the East came in the year 1241. It is from this raid that the legend developed. The legend has also been expanded, when, after World War II, Polish soldiers stopped for a night in Samarkand. There, one of the priests from the Mosque of Mahomet questioned them. "Are you from Lechistan, Lech's town?" he asked.*

"We are," the soldiers replied.

"Do us a favor! Have your trumpeters come to our marketplace and play the Hejnal at the tomb of the great Timor Khan."

The soldiers were puzzled. How did they know about the Hejnal? But, they agreed to do so. That evening, four soldiers gathered at the tomb and played the Hejnal—three times, to satisfy the anxious priest. Then, the whole city took on a festive mood.

The priests explained, "That removes the curse of our race. Seven hundred and two years ago, one of our Tartar warriors killed a Lech (Polish) trumpeter with his arrow while he played the sacred song. An old prophet said we were cursed and it would not be taken away until trumpeters from Lechistan would play that same tune before the grave of Timor Khan! Samarkand's dark days are over now. The Tartars will become a free people and live like brothers with all nations. The spirit of Genghis Khan is free once more!"

POPIEL AND THE MOUSE TOWER

It happened a long time ago. So long ago, that history was mixed with legends and folktales were thought to be true. That was when Popiel was the ruler of a tribe of people who lived in the land we now call Poland.

Popiel governed the people living around Lake Gopla, the small village was called Kruczwica. He died when his son, Popiel II, was still young, so the boy's twelve uncles helped him rule the land while he was growing up.

Popiel II was short and fat, with a small pink face and not much hair. Some people called him Chwastek, or Chwast, which means little tail or weed in Polish—not a very nice name for a ruler.

But he wasn't a very nice ruler. He had grown lazy and selfish, demanding his servants and bodyguards do everything for him. He fought with his uncles all the time, for they thought he was too strict and cruel to his people but Popiel wouldn't listen.

When he became a man, he married Ortrud, a German girl from a neighboring tribe. The tribes did this quite often, to keep everyone happy and to avert attacks from their neighbors.

Ortrud was very beautiful. But she was also very selfish and nagged Popiel for beautiful clothes and jewels. She could then show them off at large parties and banquets.

They lived in the old wooden castle in Kruszwica that Popiel's father had built. It was surrounded by a stout wooden palisade, with tall wooden watch towers. Popiel's soldiers could look out across the countryside for any approaching enemies that might want to attack them.

It wasn't long before Ortrud decided the castle was too old and that they should have a fine new one, made of brick, as they were in Germany. So German builders were brought to town and they built a new castle on the shores of Lake Goplo. It was strong and beautiful, with a wide moat and drawbridge, with tall towers and large luxurious rooms.

The building was very expensive and so were the banquets that the couple gave when they moved into their new home. So the poor peasants were taxed more and more. Popiel ordered the people to bring in all the furs from the forest animals, all the fish from the lakes and rivers, all the grain from the fields and all the honey from the hives. In this way, Popiel would be able to trade the goods with traveling caravans and have plenty of food for his family. His uncles pleaded with him…the peasants would not be able to work if they had no food. It was too much. But Popiel and Ortrud wouldn't listen.

They became more greedy and ruthless. They tricked and plundered traveling merchants and made some of them slaves. They held wild parties where Popiel would drink himself into a stupor on the golden mead the peasants made. He would shoot arrows for his own amusement. At times he would dress in armor, seize a battle axe and command a defenseless prisoner to fight him to the death.

The people lived in terror but could do nothing, for the wicked rulers were protected by special bodyguards. This group of soldiers, unlike the ordinary soldiers, were devoted to their hard-hearted master. They were staunch defenders, not out of loyalty but for the rewards they received—good food, plenty to drink, high pay and the liberty to do and take what they wanted from the peasants. They ate, drank, wenched and lived like lords.

Villagers who protested against these cruel actions were seized by the guards and thrown into the dungeons to starve or be eaten by rats. Some were even put in cages with hungry bears.

The uncles objected and asked Popiel to stop his evil ways. They were not afraid to speak out, for they held a special position, helping Popiel rule the land.

And so it was that Ortrud whispered into Popiel's ear and told him of a plan she had. She urged Popiel to call a meeting with his uncles, saying he had repented.

Ortrud planned a great banquet. The table was loaded with all kinds of food. A wild boar was roasted on a spit in the fireplace. Fresh rushes were laid on the stone floor and herbs were burned in small dishes, to give off aromatic scents. Flaming torches on the walls threw dancing lights and shadows on the long benches and tables. Music and laughter put the uncles in a good mood, as they were treated royally by Ortrud herself, as well as the servants.

Popiel acted very contritely, declaring he was sorry for all his wrong-doing. He promised to change—he would free the prisoners, feed the hungry, care for the sick and old. He promised everything—peace and good will to all. And the uncles believed him when he swore an oath, "I swear this truth, if not, let the rats eat me!"

All day long the uncles ate, drank and made merry. They talked and sang songs with Popiel and Ortrud, for they believed a new era had begun.

Ortrud rose to her feet and offered a toast to the uncles and to show her change of heart, she herself would serve her uncles and pour the wine. Around the table she went, pouring the golden mead into each goblet, whispering sweet compliments to each uncle. They all rose as Ortrud proposed her toast. "To eternal peace!" she declared.

"To eternal peace!" the uncles cried out in one voice, as they lifted their goblets high. They drank the mead in one gulp. Not one drop was left in the goblets.

The oldest uncle was the first to be seized with a searing pain in his chest. He realized he had been poisoned. "Treachery!" he cried, stumbling to his battle axe on the wall. Before he could reach it, he fell to the floor, dead.

The others soon felt the effects of the poison tearing at their insides. They were terrified and could hardly believe what was happening. One by one they fell to the floor, groaning and dying.

Popiel and Ortrud stood over them, laughing. "I promised you eternal peace; now you have it!" Ortrud squealed gleefully as their uncles groaned and cursed them.

When the last uncle lay still and dead, a silence filled the room. The couple looked at each other, triumphant in their deed. The banquet room was quiet, no sounds of music or laugher, no sounds of groaning and dying, only silence.

Suddenly voices could be heard in the courtyard. Voices crying out in fear and the sound of people running away. An army of mice had risen out of Lake Goplo and was headed straight toward the castle. The sight of the wet grey mass and the sound of thousands of scurrying feet, like the rustling of dry leaves across the cobblestones, terrified the servants, who fled in every direction.

The mice, in orderly fashion, scurried up the roadway, over the drawbridge, through the courtyard and into the banquet hall. Not stopping for a minute, they headed straight for the wicked rulers.

Popiel and his wife ran screaming from room to room, only to have the mice chase after them. The bodyguards took axes and attempted to slaughter the mice but hundreds more appeared when one was killed. They built a fire, hoping to encircle them but the mice ran through the flames, unhurt, intent on catching the greedy and murderous couple.

Not knowing what to do next, Popiel and Ortrud fled into the tower, slamming the heavy oak door shut behind them. They ran up the curved tower steps to the top room, clinging to each other in fright.

Soon the sounds of gnawing could be heard, louder and louder, until the great oak door shook and a hole developed.

One grey mouse leaped through, then another and another, rushing up the tower steps and into the room. Screams could be heard throughout the countryside, along with the excited squeals and gnawing and scampering of hundreds of mice.

Once again it was quiet. The servants and bodyguards were frozen in fright. What had happened?

The army of mice streamed down the tower steps, through

the banquet room, into the courtyard and back into the lake from which they came. As quickly as they had appeared, they disappeared into the water.

It was some days before the people began to search the castle. Warily they entered the banquet room and found the bodies of Popiel's uncles, lying untouched on the floor where they had fallen.

But in the tower, they found nothing but the clothing and jewels of Popiel and his wife. The mice had eaten them and freed the people from the oppressive rulers.

FIRST REFERENCE TO THIS POLISH TALE *is made by Muenster, in 895. He states King Popiel reigned in Polania 246 years before Christ.*

The Bavarian Geographer and the Gallus Chronicles believe the Popiels were one of the earliest ruling dynasties in the Proto-Polish land. The Popiels, probably the ruling dynasty of the Glopeani people, covered an area of Greater Poland—the lands in the Gniezno region, Lechyca, Salisia and part of the Vistulan Pomerania.

Krszwica lies between the Warta and Notec rivers, on the shores of Lake Goplo, where a Tower of Mice (built in the 15th Century) still stands today.

German folklore also has a wicked ruler and mouse tower. Wilhelm Ruland, in his The Folk Legends of the Rhine *(1902), places the story on an island in the Rhine. Just below Bingen, a Mauseturn (toll tower) was built (thirteenth Century), on a lonely island.*

Hatto, Archbishop of Mayecne commanded tolls be collected from passing ships. His evil deeds included extorting heavy taxes from his people as well. When a famine threatened the land, Hatto bought up all the corn and grain available and stored them in his granaries.

With the famine in full force, the starving people implored the Bishop to lower the price of grain, so all could afford it. To no avail.

After many months of famine and death, the people again implored the Bishop to share his grain. With hypocritical kindness, he promised them corn and brought the villagers to a huge barn, where each would receive as much as they needed.

The grateful folk rushed into the barn and when all were inside, he ordered the doors locked and set it on fire. The screams of the poor wretched people could be heard throughout the countryside.

"Listen how the mice squeal among the corn. This eternal begging is at an end at last. May the mice bite me if it's not so!"

No sooner had Hatto finished talking than thousands of mice poured out of the burning barn and filled every nook and cranny of the Bishop's palace. Seized with terror, the Bishop fled the town and went by boat to the toll tower on the island. But hordes of mice followed him. Gnawing the tower door, they rushed in and reached the Bishop in the uppermost level. The cruel man was soon devoured by the mice, so the legend goes.

Hatto is historically known for his desire for power and as the object of hatred by the people.

The story of Popiel is still told in Poland today. His drinking is stressed as the cause of his downfall—"if he drank milk, instead of piwo, he would still be alive today!"

Folklorists often symbolize the mice as outside invading forces, eliminating one ruler to make room for the next.

Polish Folk Legends

PROUD OF POTS

Long, long ago, a thousand years or possibly even more, King Wladyslaw II ruled the Polish land. He himself was a Lithuanian but Poland and Lithuania had merged to become the largest country in Europe. He decided to invite the neighboring royalty for a visit and show off the wonders of the land.

Weeks later couriers came riding through the castle gates to announce the arrival of Ernest II, the Iron Duke of Austria. Knights on horseback, wagons loaded with food and gifts, servants of all kind came parading into the castle grounds—such commotion. Everyone in the castle was excited and they looked forward to the festivities that had been planned.

Wladyslaw wanted the very best for Ernest. He wanted Austria to be a friendly neighbor. The King made arrangements to show Poland's great hospitality, the beautiful countryside and its grand castles.

In the days and weeks that followed, there were many parties and balls, with dukes and princesses from every part of the land. Hunts and games were planned every day and in the evening great tables were filled with all kinds of food and drink.

Then one day King Wladyslaw suggested a long ride in the Wielkopolska countryside. As they rode, the King pointed out the vast fields of grain, the forests with many wild animals, the bee hives and gardens of the peasants. "See how fruitful our land is!"

Ernest agreed. "Ah, yes, almost as nice as Austria!"

"Now I will show you something only the Polish land can produce," Wladyslaw exclaimed. "You shall see something you won't believe!"

Soon the carriage stopped near a lake. The two men stepped out and walked to a sandy spot where some shovels and spades lay. The King invited Ernest to take a spade and see what the soil would produce for him. Puzzled, Ernest began to move the soil around. He dug deep into the ground and heard a 'clunk'.

"You see, here our Polish soil breeds clay pots!" laughed Wladyslaw, delighted that he was able to surprise Ernest.

Ernest fell to his knees and began to push the soil away. "What are you talking about? I've heard of soil producing many things but never clay pots! What is this?" he asked, as he pulled a pot out of the soil.

With awe he examined it closely. It was a simple round pot, with two small ears for handles and around the edges were a series of lines, for decoration. It was filled with dirt.

"How wonderful!" he exclaimed.

Carefully he took out the dirt and in the bottom was a broken piece of clay, with many holes in it.

"Aha, I see you have found a piece of sieve, too. A pity it is broken. You could start making cheese in your own clay pot!"

No matter how many times Ernest asked, Wladyslaw would not tell the secret about the clay pots in the Polish soil.

WLADYSLAW MAY WELL HAVE BEEN *the first Polish archaeologist. In 1416, he ordered a "dig" and personally supervised the work in an area where local peasants insisted pots grew out of the soil. It was to this spot that he brought Ernest, knowing very well what would happen—the soil did indeed produce pots.*

It was 1933 before serious excavations took place and members of the archaeological expedition unearthed an entire, remarkable preserved, Porto-Slavic settlement that dated back many years before the time of King Wladyslaw. It was soon determined that they had located a fortified settlement on the peninsula of Lake Biskupin, over 2,500 years old.

Here, they unearthed the remains of wooden houses on eleven streets which were paved with logs. There were also manufacturing sites for stone and bronze tools as well as pottery kilns. Biskupin is now open to the public, partially reconstructed, as a unique museum of the prehistoric past of Poland.

THE EAGLE'S NEST

A thousand years ago, or maybe even more, there lived three brothers, Lech, Czech and Rus. For many years they had been content in their villages but the families grew larger and they needed more room to live.

The brothers decided to travel in different directions to search for new homes. Lech, Czech and Rus traveled with their troops for many days. They rode their horses over mountains and rivers, through forests and wild country. There were no people to be found anywhere, not a town or tiny village.

On the crest of a mountain top, they separated, each going in a different direction. Czech went to the left, Rus went to the right and Lech rode straight ahead, down the mountain and across vast plains.

One day Lech saw a splendid sight. He and his troops had come to a place where a meadow surrounded a small lake. They stopped at the edge of the meadow as a great eagle flew over their heads. It flew around in great swooping circles, then perched on its nest, high on a craggy rock.

Lech stared in awe at the beautiful sight. As the eagle spread its wings and soared into the heavens again, a ray of sunshine from the red setting sun fell on the eagle's wings, so they appeared tipped with gold, the rest of the bird was pure white.

"Here is where we will stay!" declared Lech. "Here is our new home and we will call this place Gniezno—The Eagle's Nest!"

He and his people built many houses and it became the center of his territory. They called themselves Polonians, which means field. They made a banner with a white eagle on a red field and flew it over the town of Gniezno, which became the first historical capital of Poland.

And now you know how Poland began.

THE WHITE EAGLE *became the official emblem of Poland during the reigns of Kings Wladyslaw Lokietek and Kazimierz the Great. It was set on a red banner, the while eagle having gold claws, beak and a crown on its head. It was adopted by the Piast dynasties in the 12th Century as a symbol of union within the dynasties.*

In 1945, the crown was removed by the Polish government, which was under the rule of Russia.

The three brothers are thought to represent the three main geographic divisions of the Slavs. (South—Serbs, Croats, Slovenes and Bulgarians; East—Great Russians, White Russians (Byelorussians) and Little Russians (Ukrainians); and the West—Czech, Slovaks and Poles.)

Pliny and Tacitus, Roman authors, mentioned the Slavs having settled north of the Carpathian Mountains in the first and second Century AD.

Gniezno became the capital of Mieszko I and Boleslaw Chrobry. The town was walled and fortified. Foreign traders and chronicle writers were enchanted with this beautiful town.

OPOLE

Long, long ago there weren't very many cities or towns or villages and there weren't many people living on the land either. But there were many forests, dark and thick, with huge trees, that covered most of the European continent. It was easy to get lost if you went too far into the forest and didn't know where other people were living.

A visitor to a village was always welcome and didn't have to worry about going hungry, for visitors were few and far between.

At that time there was an important prince living in the land. He would often go hunting, trumpets blaring, rifles firing, hunting the wild animals with great whoops and shouts. A very noisy affair.

One day the prince wasn't feeling well and he thought he would like to be by himself; a little peace and quiet would make his throbbing head feel better, he thought. And so he climbed up on his horse, pulled his cap down over his ears and set out for the cool forest paths. He rode and rode until he was tired. In a cool dark glen he rested and fell asleep and when he awoke, his head felt better and he was eager to be on his way.

He rode on again, looking for familiar landmarks in the deep woods but he couldn't find anything that looked familiar. Trees and more trees, that was all.

All at once he realized he was lost. A prince lost in the forest would never do. He blew his trumpet and called and called but there was no one to hear him.

On and on he rode and thought he must be riding in circles, for he had never gotten lost before. The trees and bushes were like a jungle, so thick and dark and tangled that he often had to lead his horse through the thickets. More than once he stumbled and fell as the vines and briars caught his feet. Staggering about, he kept calling but no one answered.

Suddenly he saw some light through the trees and soon a silvery mist could be seen. Excited, he hurried toward the light. There appeared a clearing in the forest, wide and beautiful and in the middle, a river flowed.

The prince was so happy, he ran joyously through the meadow and called "O pole!"—over and over again. Now he knew where he was; the river was the Odra and his castle was not far away. His courier was riding in the field, searching for the prince. Together they rode back to the castle and the prince, remembering his shout of joy, built a town in the field by the Odra and named it after his call, "OPOLE!"

OPOLE CAN BE FOUND *on maps as early as AD 989, the unification of the Polish slate by Mieszko I. While it never became a stronghold for Mieszko, as were Gniezno and Poznan, it served as an important trading post. Archaeologists have discovered goods from China, Japan, Korea and India during excavations at Opole. The prince laid out his town with log-paved streets, inns for travelers who brought a wealth of goods for exchange and a rampart that surrounded the town.*

Opole became the capital of the Piast Dukedom between 1201 and 1532. The town came under the control of the Bohemians, Hapsburgs, Prussians and Germans before being returned to Poland in 1945. Today, it is a city of over 90,000.

Polish Folk Legends

ORIGINS OF THE PIAST DYNASTY

I'll tell you a tale about the beginnings of the Slavic nation under the peasant dynasty of the Piasts.

One day two travelers came upon a clearing with a *grody.* That's a small village surrounded by a stout wooden wall to protect the prince and inhabitants from invading tribes. The travelers were happy to see the *grody,* for they had been traveling all day and were hungry and tired.

But when they came to the gate, the townspeople wouldn't let them in. How were they to know if they could trust these strangers?

"Go away," they said. "We're getting ready to have a party and don't want any trouble! Tomorrow there will be a 'shearing' for our Prince's son!"

Now a 'shearing' in those days was a very special event. Up to the age of seven, boys and girls were under the care of their mother. But when they reached seven, they were expected to do more work and take on more responsibilities. A boy's hair was cut for the first time. He was given a name and often, his first pair of trousers. His father would teach him how to tend cattle, how to hunt with a bow and arrow and the work of other men. He was no longer thought of as a child.

Parents would invite their friends to the celebration and provide as lavish a feast as they could afford. It was a time to stop their daily chores and enjoy themselves.

Sadly the two travelers turned away from the village and continued on their journey. Soon they came to a small cottage with a thatched roof, snuggled close to the ground. It stood near plowed fields with a forest in the distance. There were some people working in the garden and a pig roasting over an open pit. When they saw the strangers approaching, they stopped their work and greeted them.

"Can we rest here and get a drink?" asked one of the men.

"Of course," answered the gardener. "Come and sit by the well and my wife will draw some water."

The weary men rested on a bench as the woman drew a bucket of water.

"This is my wife, Rzepka and I am Piast, plowman for the Prince," said the man. "Our son, here, will be sheared tomorrow and we are getting ready for the celebration."

Even though there was still work to do, Piast and Rzepka sat and visited with the strangers, for they were polite and kind to all people. Piast told them how he worked the fields for their prince and still tilled some land for his family, how he hunted in the forests with a bow and arrow and how he and Rzepka brought up their son to respect the land and its people.

The strangers were impressed by this couple and listened to the story of their life. Finally one of them said, "Do you have anything stronger to drink?" as he held up his cup.

Piast was surprised at the request and thought about his barrel of miod fermenting for the shearing party. "We have been saving our miod for the celebration, but we will give you some," he said and filled their cups with the drink. The barrel remained as full as before and Piast wondered about that to himself.

Night fell and the two travelers agreed to stay the night and join in the next day's feast. Bread was baked with grain that Piast had grown in the fields and Rzepka had ground into flour.

Rzepka had also made her son a pair of trousers from woolen cloth she had woven herself. She even managed to brighten parts of the trousers with a red dye she made from insects in the field. A sheepskin coat was finished, for the boy to wear on cold days when he tended the cattle in the hills.

They were very busy. Soon their friends arrived and helped put the dishes of food on the long board-table. Rzepka cut up the roasted pig and it filled many dishes—more than ever before. The guests were amazed at how delicious it tasted and how much there was. When Piast poured out the drinks, the barrel never emptied. The couple wondered what was happening.

After the feast, the boy's hair was cut by one of their friends. As the long hair fell to the ground, Rzepka wept. No longer would she have her baby. Piast gave him the name, Ziemowit, then he gave the boy the trousers and coat.

Ziemowit put on the trousers for the first time and tucked in his long shirt. He looked like a fine sturdy young man and his parents were very proud of him.

The travelers said to Piast: "We are total strangers and yet you have been kind and generous to us. In your wisdom, you will gain honor and glory for your descendants. Great things will come to this family!"

And so it was that the dynasty of the Piasts began, from humble peasant origins, to rule the land in the Gniezno-Kruszwicz-Poznani area. Ziemowit grew to be a brave and true leader and when Popiel died, the people chose him to be their Prince, for he was honored and loved by all.

THE "SHEARING" IS AN ANCIENT *pagan custom that prevailed in the land and can be compared to the many initiation customs throughout the world of young people coming into adulthood. Following a "cutting" of the body, the person was accepted as a full part of the community.*

The Piast dynasty, beginning with the legendary couple, is historically recognized with Ziemomysl (c963) whose son, Mieszko became the first ruler to accept Christianity.

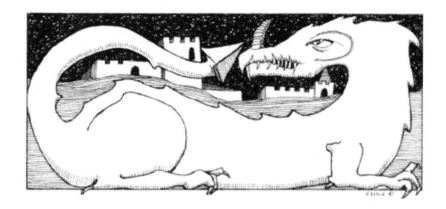

KRAK AND THE DRAGON

Long, long ago there was a small settlement of wooden huts along the banks of the Wisla river. The river curved around a hill and in this hill was a cave. The people knew about the cave; there was a dragon—a monster—living there, who came out when he was hungry. He ate everything in his path, so you can be sure there were not many people who wanted to live on that side of the hill.

The dragon would come out of the cave and roar and tongues of fire would shoot out of his mouth. He would shake the hillside and tear up the trees and bushes, searching for food. He often found some of the villager's sheep, dogs, or pigs and would swallow them whole.

His long sharp teeth and fiery eyes frightened even the bravest of men. His green scaly skin shone in the sunshine as he swam in the river and sprayed water high in the air.

One day the villagers got together. "We can't take this any longer! Doesn't anyone have any ideas how to get rid of the dragon? We will soon starve or be eaten ourselves if we don't do something. But what?"

The people grumbled to themselves. It was true, something had to be done. Men had tried to kill the dragon with axes before but no blow could penetrate through the thick scales and some had died while trying.

Among the villagers was a man called Krak. He knew how to heal people and would mix herbs and potions for the sick. He was always willing to help people and give good advice. The other villagers respected him.

"Krak, what do you think? Can you find a way to get rid of the dragon?"

Krak, of course, had been worried about the dragon, too. "Well," he said, "I have been thinking of something that might work."

The people gathered about him while he told them of his plan. "Bring me a young sheep," he said, "and I will start."

In his small hut, he began looking through his many crocks. Soon he was mixing a batch of thick yellow paste. It smelled awful and the villagers backed out of the hut when they brought him the animal they had just slaughtered. Krak quickly cut open its belly and poured the thick yellow paste inside. He rubbed whatever was left all over the head and legs of the animal. He called the men to help him and together they carried the sheep up the hill, going as far as the mouth of the cave and then threw it into the dark hole.

Breathless and anxious, they scrambled back down the hill and hid in some bushes and waited. Suddenly, the dragon rushed out of the cave, roaring and bellowing. He ran to the river and drank and drank and drank. The dinner tossed into his cave came with a dressing of sulfur and the inside of the dragon's stomach seemed to be on fire. The cool water from the Wisla seemed to help for a while—while he drank. So the dragon continued to drink.

The villagers, even from a distance, could see something strange happening. The dragon was getting bigger. He drank so much he began to swell. But he couldn't stop drinking, for the fire in his belly wouldn't go away. Suddenly, there was a great explosion and the dragon burst into a million pieces.

Well, of course, the people were very happy. Now, they had nothing to fear. Soon they built a fort there, so they might all live together and they chose Krak for their leader. The land prospered under the rule of Krak, the village grew bigger and bigger around the hill and became known as Krakow.

WAWEL HILL IS A ROCKY *limestone section looking over the banks of the Wisla (Vistula). From the 8th to 10th Century, it was the sight of a fort established by the Vistulans. Archaeologists have discovered remains of a pre-Romanesque rotunda and a tenth Century palace (grody). Today, the hill contains many treasures and castles of past rulers that are visited by countless people. At the foot of the hill, people also visit the cave of the dragon, and the dragon himself, who stands tall and shoots fiery flames from his mouth—no doubt some remnants of his last meal.*

QUEEN WANDA

When Krak had killed the dragon that lived in the cave in Wawel Hill, the people were very grateful and they asked him to be their leader. He guided the tribe and ruled for a very long time. They developed their settlement on the river, farmed, fished and hunted and protected their territory from invaders. When he grew old and died, it was decided his oldest son, also named Krak, would be their next ruler. But his younger brother wanted the job and one day when no one was looking, Lech killed his brother. But Lech didn't last very long, for the villagers found Krak's body and realized what Lech had done. They forced him to leave the protection of the settlement and flee into the forest.

Then the villagers and councilors gathered in the old wooden fortress. "Now, what shall we do? Who will guide us?"

A councilor spoke up, "Krak had three children. His daughter Wanda is very wise and kind!"

"What! Shall we have a woman rule us?"

"Well, she always sat by her father at meetings and everyone likes her and besides, what else can we do?"

Everyone agreed she was good and brave and just.

"So be it," the oldest councilor declared. "She will be our Queen!"

When Wanda heard this, she trembled at the thought of guiding and protecting the people. They assured her she was the one they wanted and encouraged her to take the throne. And so it was that the land of Krak had a woman for a leader.

Wanda worked hard to make the people happy and safe. In those days there were foreigners who brought goods to trade and were friendly but there were also foreigners who saw the lovely fields and forests that surrounded the settlement and tried to claim it for their own. It is said that Wanda, herself, would lead her soldiers in the battlefields. She inspired them with her bravery and they successfully defeated many foes.

Wanda's fame spread far and wide and soon a German prince, Rytygier, heard of her beauty and bravery. Even more, he knew the lands she ruled were fruitful and rich. He sent a message to Wanda, asking for her hand in marriage.

It was a marriage proposal but also a demand to surrender to the prince. He wanted the lands of Polani for her dowry and threatened to fight for her and her lands if she refused.

Wanda was very upset. She didn't want to marry a German prince. She didn't want to give him the Polish lands and the people that trusted her. Rytygier's armies were very large; Wanda's small band of warriors would certainly be defeated. If she had not been so beautiful, brave and wise, Rytygier might not have noticed her or the fertile lands. She felt she was responsible for this ultimatum.

"I love my land and my people," she cried to the councilors. "I can't give in to the prince's demand!"

And she retreated to her room trying to decide what to do.

The next day, she prepared a huge banquet for all her people and called them together. She told them how much she loved them and would do anything to protect them. Then she urged them to come to the table and enjoy the feast. Soon the old fortress was full of partying people. No one looked for her after she had greeted them. In the cool of the evening she again retired to her room, where she prayed to God to grant her people freedom from the German prince in return for her life.

She had decided to sacrifice herself, rather than marry Rytygier and surrender her lands to the German! And in the darkness, she threw herself into the Vistula and drowned.

It was many days before her body was found and then she was buried with honor. The people honored her by heaping mounds of dirt on her grave until it became as large as her father's. Her mound is called Mogila and is there to this day.

FIRST TOLD BY *Bishop Vincent Kadlubek in 1206, the Wanda legend has been told and retold many times through the centuries. It symbolizes the folk philosophy of good overcoming evil. The name Wanda, (pronounced "Vanda" in Polish), is linked to the great mother of rivers, the Vistula. Every child in Poland, learning of the bravery of Wanda, develops a respect and love for their land.*

THE ENCHANTED EEL

For ages, the blue waves of the Baltic have washed upon the shores of Puck. Foreign ships would unload their goods at the Puck harbor and carry away lumps of amber, coal and smoked fish in exchange. There was a great wealth of fish in the Bay of Gdansk especially salmon and eel. When Polish fishermen returned from a day's fishing, their boats were always overloaded with fish.

From this abundance of fish and from the trade of foreign merchants, the wealth of Puck grew day by day. The townspeople were very proud of their town but they were upset because they had no coat of arms.

A meeting of the council was called. "Mayor, we need to have a coat of arms to present to our visitors. Our town deserves one, now that we are growing so important!"

The councilmen put their heads together. "What sort of coat of arms?" they asked one another.

"Oh, a very special one! Magnificent. As befitting such a noble town," one of the councilmen answered. Everyone agreed. But no one could think of anything really beautiful. Nothing seemed good enough.

One day when they were having their usual discussion, a sailor came running into the town hall. "There's a ship from a distant land and it has the strangest animal aboard."

The noblemen, with the mayor in the lead, ran to the harbor. The sailor was right. On board the foreign ship in a large strong cage was this unknown animal. It looked terrible and beautiful at the same time. It had a huge fawn mane and its roar sounded like thunder.

141

"What is this animal called?" they asked.

"He is called lion and is king of animals," the shipmaster answered.

"He is called lion and is king of animals," repeated the delighted noblemen.

They looked at one another and at once decided: "Here is an animal worthy to appear in the arms of our town!"

But as soon as this was said, the strangest thing happened. A huge salmon emerged from the waves and spoke. "Ho, good noblemen! What is this? Am I worse than the lion? It is true he is fine and fearsome but don't you owe your wealth and fame to the salmon? Why don't you have me in the coat of arms for the town?"

The Puck people were thoughtful. "Ach," murmured the noblemen. "What shall we do? It's a pity to give up the beautiful lion but the salmon will be angered.''

"Well," the sailor said timidly, "you could put the salmon and lion together in the coat."

The noblemen put their heads together once more and decided, "Let the lion and salmon be together in the coat of arms of Puck!"

The words were hardly spoken when the waves washed the shore, bringing up an eel. "Wait, gentlemen!" it exclaimed resentfully. "Am I worse than the salmon? Your catch of eel is equally good. And I want to be in your coat of arms!"

"We can't have you there, that would be too many," explained the noblemen. "Please don't insist, dear eel."

"So that's how it is!" stormed the eel. "This is your gratitude? Then I, together with my whole family will swim elsewhere and never come back!"

The noblemen were frightened. What would they do without the eels? What would they eat and what would they sell?

Quick as a wink, the noblemen grasped the eel and chained him to the Puck shore.

And so he remains there with his whole family, forever. And in the coat of arms of Puck you can see the lion and the salmon fighting over supremacy.

PUCK IS LOCATED *in the crook of arm that juts into the Gdansk Bay. It is sheltered from the rough seas of the Baltic by this spit of land and at one time, was an important fishing village. Its coat of arms still remains.*

GOLDEN QUEEN OF THE SEASHORE

A million years ago, or maybe even more, the earth was full of animals and flowers, birds and trees and they could all talk. The mighty Oak was King of all the trees.

One day the trees had a meeting. "Oak," they said, "we would like to travel all over the earth and choose our own place to live." After some thought, the Oak agreed. "Fine," he said, "Go out into the world and see what you will see. In a year, I will visit and see how each of you is doing."

And so they did.

When a year had gone by, the Oak King went about the land, visiting all the trees. He came at once upon the Willows and Poplars by the roadside. "How are you doing?" he asked.

"Very well, thank you," they nodded in a chorus. The Oak went on. In the village, he met the merry Lindens. They too were happy with their chosen home. On a hillside, he came upon the sturdy Beeches. They bowed to him in the bright meadows. And higher up the hill were the Firs and Spruces.

And so King Oak traveled throughout the land, greeting all the trees. Then he came to the sea. I'll turn back now, he thought. No use going further. Nothing but barren land and sand here. Surely no trees would choose to grow here.

"Of course they have," a voice called. "Oak, do go a little further and you will meet the bravest of your subjects and my dearest friend." It was a tall cattail calling.

What a surprise for the Oak when he went past the sand dune and saw a green wood where once there was only barren land. Grasses and wild berries grew in the shade of the trees. Farther off, flowering new meadows and above, birds sang merrily.

"Who could have managed the barrens so well?" the Oak marveled.

"The Pine did," the cattail answered. "Thanks to it, we now have a fine piece of land, instead of flying sands tossed by the wild wind and sea." The Oak looked lovingly at the Pine. It was still young and strong but bent and twisted by the sea winds that blew day and night. Its roots had difficulty anchoring into the poor soil, so close to the seashore.

"Pine, you have chosen the poorest soil and the hardest life. You are so very brave. Because of your courage, I name you Queen of the Seashore. Your tears shall become gems to the people forever. The sap from your body will drop into the sea and congeal into precious gems. When they are tossed ashore and people find them, they will treasure the sacrifice you have made for their sake."

"So be it!' cried the cattail.

And so it was and so it is to this very day.

FOR THOUSANDS OF YEARS *amber has been a baffling matter. It has the hue and brilliance to make it look like gold and at the same time, it is light and translucent. The congealed sap of primeval conifers, through heat and pressure over millions of years polymerized the resin, transforming it into the gem we treasure. Amber that includes an insect or flower is several times more valuable than clear amber and at one time, it was believed to be placed there by witchcraft.*

Everything that is made of amber is iridescent, glitters and reflects the light. Merchants from ancient Rome established trade routes to the Baltic in search of amber, believing it to hold magical powers.

Amber was used for barter by fishermen for hundreds of years until the Teutonic knights obtained exclusive rights to collect the amber. They stationed guards along the coast to make sure the fishermen handed over the amber. They were paid in salt and coins. King Kazimierz the Jagiellonian later declared amber to be freed.

Today, as long ago, amber is considered a gem worth having.

TREASURE KEEPERS

"Please give me some bread!"

Karol had just started to eat his lunch when he heard the request. He lifted his lantern and swung it around the dark coal mine. He could only see the black walls of coal and stone, his cart and pick-axe. Nothing more.

"Now I'm hearing things," he thought. It was Karol's first day as a coal miner and other workers had sent him to the poorest shaft to dig for coal. He worked all morning and only had a small bucket of coal to show for all that time. He sighed as he took a bite of his lunch.

"Please give me some bread," a small voice called.

Suddenly a fat gray mouse jumped in front of Karol, sitting up as if to beg for food.

Karol broke off a piece of his bread and tossed it to the mouse and laughed. "For a moment I thought I heard you talking!"

The mouse munched the bread, every crumb and asked for more.

"Sorry, that's all I have! but tomorrow I'll bring you some more." He hardly finished talking when the mouse jumped closer and in a flash, changed into an elf. Karol had heard of elves but he was surprised to really see one. Everyone in Poland told stories about the *Skarbnik*. They lived underground and guarded the earth's treasures. Sometime they played tricks on the miners, changing into any shape or form and popping up in the most unexpected place. They could bring good luck, too. But usually it was bad luck and the miners always tried to avoid any nook or cranny where the Skarbnik might be hiding and never whistled in the mines. That irritated the Skarbnik most of all.

The little elf danced up and down in front of Karol. He was almost two-feet tall and his beard was almost as long. He wore a long pointed cap on his head and his clothes were as black as coal.

"So," he laughed, "They put you to work here."

"Yes and so far I haven't had much luck," sighed the young miner.

"Well, I'll help you, since you shared your bread with me." And the elf pointed to a place to dig. Strangely enough, each blow of the pick-axe brought forth an avalanche of pure coal. Karol stopped to thank the elf but all he saw was a little mouse scurry away. Before the day ended, Karol had filled his coal cart with ten times more coal than he was expected to collect.

The next day, the mouse appeared again.

"Please give me some bread!" Again, Karol gave him some and when he had finished nibbling up every crumb, he jumped on the coal-cart and changed into a Skarbnik again.

"For being such a good fellow and sharing your bread, I will help you every day! But from now on, I want a share of your earnings, not your bread!" declared the elf. "One half for you and one half for me!''

Karol agreed, for without the elf's help, he had little success in finding coal.

All day long he chipped away at the walls of the mine, wherever the Skarbnik pointed. Chucks of coal broke off from the pick-axe blows. Again, the coal cart was filled before the day ended.

At the end of the week, he received a very large sum of money and the other miners were amazed. "What will you do with all that money?" they asked. "Let's celebrate! Come to the tavern!"

"No," said Karol and he quietly went back into the mine, down the shaft were he had been working.

"Skarbnik, I am here," he called, as he swung his lantern around the dark shaft. He found Skarbnik sitting on a plank that had been thrown over a deep hole. The elf was sitting right in the middle.

"Come here and join me," Skarbnik called.

Karol eased himself across the plank until he was sitting next to the elf. He took a bag of coins from his pocket and began to divide the money into two equal piles on the plank. Finally, there was one coin left and he put it in Skarbnik's pile.

"That's for you," he said. "Everything I earned was due to your help, anyway!"

Skarbnik danced up and down on the plank for joy. "Oh, I waited a long time to hear that! You're a lucky fellow."

"Why? That was our agreement."

"Yes, we agreed to share the money. But you went a little farther. You gave me the last coin. If you hadn't done that, you would be at the bottom of this hole right now—like so many before you!"

Karol was more puzzled than ever.

"I'll tell you a secret," said the elf. "For a long time I've been looking for an honest man, with a kind heart. The miners before you were greedy and their hands trembled at the sight of money. They always took the last coin for themselves, or even worse, tried to keep it all! They perished in the hole for not keeping their promise! But you're a good fellow. Your work will always be easy and you won't have any accidents. Your axe will always strike coal!"

In a wink of the eye the elf changed back into a fat gray mouse and scurried off the plank into the darkness. Karol gather up his pile of coins and went home. When he got there, he found another pile of coins on the table—Skarbnik's coins, waiting for him.

Every year Karol celebrates Barburka. Miner's Day, by leaving his lunch in a small corner of a mine shaft!

BARBURKA IS CELEBRATED ON DECEMBER 4 *by the entire country. It is considered one of the traditional holidays. It is also St. Barbara's Day and she is the patron saint of miners.*

The nation takes time to honor the miners who work so hard supplying the basic necessities of life. Mining in Poland began centuries ago. Salt in Wieliczka, silver and lead in Olkusz, coal in Silesia, dolomite in Kujawa, copper in Lublin and sulfur in Tarnobrzeg. The beginnings of mining reach back to the first Century, B. C., when red iron ore was extracted from the Polish soil.

Following World War II, Poland became the fourth largest coal-producing nation in the world.

Many superstitions surround the mining industry, including the Skarbnik and the Pustecki. mythical figures who beat lazy miners and steal the lamps of sleeping miners.

THE TRUE STORY OF JANOSIK,
Robber-Chieftain of the Tatras

Janosik came from the small village of Liptow, in the foot-hills of the Tatra Mountains. When he was a young lad he was sent to school in Krakow. Now, at that time, there wasn't any easy way to travel. There weren't any trains or buses, not even a decent road, only footpaths and trails through the valley and hills to the mountains.

It took two days or more to travel from Krakow and if you got lost in the forest and didn't remember to bring along some food, you would surely starve to death.

Well, after many years of studying in Krakow, Janosik decided to go home for a visit. He started off toward the forests and hills of home. By the end of the day, he was deep in the forest and realized he was lost.

He was very hungry but being an intelligent lad, he had brought along a bundle of food. He sat down and ate while he thought about finding his way home.

When he was finished eating he climbed a tall tree and looked about, hoping to recognize some point, or see a for-ester's cabin. He couldn't see anything and was about to climb down when a small twinkle caught his eye. He stared and stared at the tiny twinkling light, far off in the distance. Maybe, he thought it's a woodcutter's cabin. Maybe he will let me stay the night and direct me home in the morning.

And so with high hopes, he started off in the direction of the light. He walked and walked and walked, always straining his eyes for that small light in the darkness. All night long he walked and in the early light of the morn he saw a clearing through the fir trees. There in the clearing was a small hut.

It was almost falling down but a light was still shining from the window. He went inside and there stood an old woman at the stove. She had a very long crooked nose and eyes that were as large as a cow's—a frightening sight but Janosik was too tired to be frightened.

The old woman stared at him, surprised to see someone in the cabin. "What are you doing here?" she asked. "Where did you come from? How did you get here? Who are you?" She was very upset to see him there and didn't even give him time to answer.

Janosik sat down on the floor. "I'm so tired, please let me sleep here for a while and I will be on my way to Liptow." But he thought to himself, I think I've come upon a robber's den.

The old woman snorted, "Eh, this is the robbers' territory! Now that you've come here and found us, you can't leave. No one leaves this secret place. Only the robbers come and go. When they find you, they will beat you!"

But still, she felt sorry for the lad, for he looked so tired. She gave him something to eat—turnips and bread and cold water to drink. When he ate it all, she sent him to the top of the stove to sleep and gave him a blanket to cover himself. In that warm place he soon fell fast asleep.

In a little while the robbers returned from a night of plunder. They dropped their bags of money and goods on the table and called to the old woman for something to eat.

The chieftain sniffed and looked around. "Tfe, tfe, tfe, I smell a man!" he called out and started to look around. He spied Janosik behind the stove and pulled a hatchet from his holster, ready to beat the poor lad.

"Wait, let him go," cried out the old woman. "He's a nice sort of lad. He walked through the forest all night. He surely must be a brave soul to do that! Perhaps we can make a robber out of him."

The robbers ate their meal as they listened to the old woman. "We will test him. If he can hold three hot coals on his bare chest without moving a muscle or crying out, he will surely make a great robber, maybe even become a robber-chieftain some day! I will call my sisters and we'll test him and we won't give him any help, either!" And the robbers agreed.

Janosik heard all of this, for he really wasn't asleep. Oh Boze, he thought, what am I to do now?

The three sisters drew their long dark dresses round themselves and huddled for a conference. They were really witches and could conjure up magical powers and spells. "What are we to do?" asked the youngest.

And the oldest, the one that had given Janosik something to eat, said: "I told the robbers we would put him to a test. We have here on the stove a truly remarkable fellow. I know it. But we must test him for the robbers. Each of us will drop a burning hot coal on his chest and if he doesn't cry out or move, he will have passed the test."

"Ah, yes," they nodded and spit on the ground three times to seal their agreement.

"But if he passes the test, what will we do?" the middle one asked.

"Listen," said the oldest, "if that happens, we will make him a robber-chieftain. And you know the three things he will need to be a great robber-chief!"

"Ah. yes," they nodded.

The youngest said, "I will make him a suit of clothes so thick, no bullet will pass through."

And the other said, "I will make him a leather belt to protect him from harm."

And the oldest said, "And I will give him a marvelous *ciupaga*—a splendid mountaineer's long-handled hatchet that will do his bidding for a hundred years!"

And so it was that the three witches tested Janosik. One by one they dropped a burning hot coal on his bare chest. He wanted to scream out but he stifled the scream in his throat and steeled himself not to move a muscle. He passed the test, just as the old witch had predicted.

Now the witches had a task, for the three gifts had to be made and given before three days had gone by. So off they went, each in her own direction to do her work.

And in two days they were finished and went to look for Janosik. He was huddled on top of the stove again, tending to his wounded chest.

"Come down," they called. "We have some great gifts for you. You will be the best robber-chief there is, for we are going to give you some magical powers. With these you will be able to help yourself and other people in need."

And the youngest gave him his suit of clothes. "I have made you a fine suit of clothes. It is warm and thick. No harm will come to you while you wear it and no sword can break through the cloth."

The middle one said, "I have made you a fine wide leather belt to fit snug about your waist. It will give you great knowledge, so you will be a leader among men."

And the oldest, the one who had given him something to eat and a place to sleep said, "Here is a special ciupaga. This hatchet will do as you command. It will be a good companion in fights, it will chop through the thickest wood, it will pull you up the steepest mountain.

"As long as you have this belt and clothing and ciupaga, you will be safe from harm. You will be Janosik, the most famous robber-chief of the Tatra Mountains."

Janosik put on the clothes and belt and took the ciupaga in his hand. He felt courage go through his body. He felt brave and strong.

The witches sent him on his way. "Go, Janosik, to Bialej Skale. Go and look at it three times, then with your ciupaga strike the rock three times. It will open up. In the cave make a cross on the ground and spit three times, saying, "No one else will open you, no one else will take your treasures." He did as he was told. He found a bag full of gold, which he gave to the poor in Liptow.

Janosik no longer lives but the three witches to this very day guard the secret place of Bialej Skale. Soldiers come from time to time and dig a hole and lay dynamite, looking for the treasure. But the cave doesn't open and no one is successful in their search. Only Janosik—and the three witches—know where the treasure lies.

JANOSIK IS THE LEGENDARY HERO, *strong defender of the poor and the Robin Hood of Poland. The Podhale and Slowacki regions claim him as their own. But he is a hero to the people of Czechoslovakia, Poland and Hungary.*

Living in the wild treacherous Tatra Mountains, he is an outlaw whose acts are incredible, who defends the poor and oppressed, who lives a magical life. Tradition has it that three witches gave him magical powers with a shirt, belt and ciupaga.

His tale was first recorded in 1713.

SAINT STANISLAW

Long, long ago when Prince Boleslaw ruled the land, the pope named Stanislaw of Szczepanow as Bishop of Krakow. For a long time, Stanislaw had led the people of Krakow, teaching, praying and helping them and people loved him very much. When he was appointed Bishop, a man named Piotrowin sold his estate to the diocese of Krakow and Stanislaw acted as agent. When the gentleman died, his family complained that the Bishop never paid for the property. The case was taken to the King, where Stanislaw declared he had paid the man but had no written proof.

"Well," said Boleslaw, "How are we to settle the matter?"

"Give me three days and I will bring you proof," begged the Bishop.

When it was granted, he and a group of clergy went to the place where Piotrowin was buried and prayed at his grave. They prayed for three days and then Stanislaw ordered the churchmen to open his grave.

Then, standing before it he called out to the dead man, "In the name of the Father, the Son and Holy Ghost, come forth." The dead man rose from the grave and stood before them.

"Come," beckoned the Bishop. And he led the dead man to the King.

"Tell him," the Bishop simply said.

And Piotrowin solemnly declared he had been paid in full for his property by the Bishop. So the matter was settled and Stanislaw became even more beloved by the people.

Bishop Stanislaw continued to preach the laws of the church, urging men to be brothers. The King, on the other hand, demanded loyalty from his subjects but cared little for their welfare. No amount of urging could get the King to change his ways.

The Bishop continued to be a thorn in Boleslaw's side and soon he ordered his priests to stop saying the divine office if the King entered the church.

Boleslaw was so furious at this insult, he decided something had to be done. On May 8, 1079, he confronted the Bishop on the steps of the *Skala* church, in the outskirts of Krakow.

He ordered his guards to kill him but they were afraid to hurt the saintly man. The King then drew his sword and murdered the saint himself, chopping his body into pieces.

But a divine light shone down on the scene and restored his body to a whole again.

Amidst much mourning for the holy man, Bishop Stanislaw was buried in the chapel of the church.

Boleslaw was so hated for his act against the saintly man that he was forced into exile shortly after the murder and died two years later.

THE MARTYRDOM OF *Stanislaw is observed on the national feast day. May 8. He is revered as the Patron Saint of Poland, being the first Polish saint. A second feast day is celebrated in the Krakow area on September 27, to commemorate the transfer of his body from the chapel to the Cathedral crypt in Wawel castle.*

A generation later, during canonization, it was recorded: "Just as the power of God reunited the holy remains of the martyred Stanislaw to a whole so in the Future it will restore the divided kingdom of Poland to its former unity."

Generally, it is accepted that Saint Stanislaw has become a symbol of the Church's independence from the nation. This independence from the ruling powers of the land remain as strong today as it was a thousand years ago.

BARBARA'S GHOST

When the wife of King Sigismund Augustus died, he was distressed and melancholy. He loved Barbara even more than he had loved his first wife and was very upset. He hated to let her go and prostrated himself on her grave. All the riches in the world couldn't help him, he thought. But then he remembered something.

Many people had been talking about the study of alchemy and the art of black magic that had been going on at the Academy. I will call the finest and most knowledgeable men to help me, he thought.

"Who is the most knowledgeable, the most famous in our Academy?" he asked his courtiers.

"Your Honor, we have those who are studying the unknown," a courtier answered. "There are many learned men from all over Europe who are here. There is Doctor Faust, Nicolaus Copernicus, Pan Twardowski, Aleksander Seton and Michal Sedziwoj, to name a few. Whom do you wish to see?"

The King thought for a while. He had heard of and even had visits with many of these men who sought to known the unknown. But one name above all the others was the most famous. "Call Pan Twardowski," he replied. "He, above all, will have the powers I need."

When Twardowski arrived, they sat and quietly talked about Queen Barbara Radziwill for a long time. Indeed, the King had seldom left the room of his beloved wife. "If only I could keep her with me," he moaned. "If only I could keep her."

Twardowski said, "It is a difficult proposition," he sighed. "But I will try to awaken her spirit, her ghost. But where her soul is at this time, I don't know."

He instructed the King to sit quietly in his chair and not move, no matter what happened. Then he concentrated his mental powers on the spirit of Barbara.

After a long time, there was a movement in the room, a light. The King's heart quickened. What could it be?

"Behold," Twardowski said softly. And there before them floating in the air was an apparition of Barbara, with color in her cheeks and her long garment falling softly about her.

Astonished and delighted, the King could hardly contain himself. "You have raised Barbara's ghost," he cried.

"Oh, my Barbara, how good it is to see you once more!" And with that he rose and went to embrace her, to put his arms around his beloved.

"You must not!" Twardowski cried out, trying to stop him. But it was too late. She disappeared as quickly as she had appeared!

IN REFERENCE TO THE REALITY OF THE EVENT, *"raising the ghost", the Royal Vice Chancellor Bishop Krasinski and courtiers Jerzy and Mikolaj Minszchowie, helped conduct the séance in the sacristy of the church of Wegrow.*

King Sigismund Augustus ruled from 1548-1572 and Barbara was his second wife, (1520-51). He was the last ruler of the Jagiellon dynasty.

Polish Folk Legends

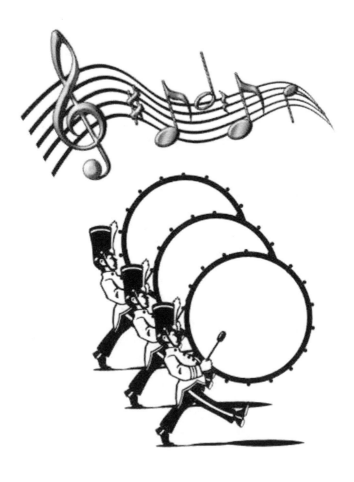

"JESZCZE POLSKA NIE ZGINELA"

Wybicki rode into town on horseback, hot, tired and dusty. It had been a long ride—from Paris, to Italy, over the Alps and into the small town of Reggio. All about him were troops and horses, wagons and ammunition, banners and tent-barracks and above all, the noise of neighing horses, shouting men and trumpet calls.

He rode through the groups, studying battle-weary faces until he found what he had come for—the headquarters of the Polish Legion.

He sucked in his breath and sat taller in his saddle when he saw the Polish flag in the national colors flying high. The sight of the flag and the men in their Polish uniforms with the silver eagles and a patch on their sleeve—"Free Men Are Brothers"— brought tears to his eyes.

Here, on foreign soil was a part of Poland; here the flag could fly, although it could no longer fly over the Polish land. The poet-soldier was deeply impressed.

It was summer, July 7, 1797 and Jozef Wybicki had arrived to join General Henryk Dabrowski and his Polish legions. They, along with many others, had been outlawed by the Russians after the Partitions of Poland. Now, men without a country, they prepared to fight under Napoleon, for the freedom of Poland and all oppressed nations.

In January Dabrowski had received permission from Napoleon to form his own Polish Legion and fight under the Emperor's command. Dabrowski believed in Napoleon and felt when the time was right, they would march into Poland and regain its independence.

Men from all walks of life came to Italy to join Dabrowski and train for war. Prisoners and deserters from the Austrian army, peasants and hundreds of émigrés who had taken part in earlier revolutions and wanted more than anything to regain their freedom and independence. Soon there were enough men to form three legions and they were ready to fight under the French flag.

That evening Jozef Wybicki sat down and putting his feelings into words, composed a song. In it he expressed the hope that the Legions, just as the armies of Napoleon, would march into Poland with General Dabrowski. With the force of the sword, they would bring independence to their homeland.

He sung "Song of the Polish Legions in Italy" at a reception for senior officers at General Dabrowski's headquarters. And then on July 16 it was played for the first time by the Military Band of the Polish Legion in Piazza Maggiore in Reggio, at a parade held in celebration of the proclamation of the Cisalpine Republic.

And that is how Poland's national anthem originated. *Jeszce Polska nie zginela...* first called the Dabrowski Mazurka, became popular immediately. The tune, like many folk songs, was lively and full of rhythm. The text, simple and reflecting the mood of the time, uplifting in spirit and promising hope of better times, became dear to the soldiers' hearts.

Florence Waszkelewicz Clowes

Jeszce Polska nie zginela
kiedy my zyjemy.
Co nam obca przemoc wziela moca odbierzemy.

Marsz, marsz, Dabrowski
Z ziemi Wloskiej do Polskiej.
Za twoim przewodem
Zlaczym sie znarodem.

Przejdziem Wiste, przejdziem Warte,
Bedziem Polakami.
Dal nam przyklad Bonaparte
Jak zwyciezyc mamy.
Marsz, marsz Dabrowski. . .

Poland has not yet perished
As long as we shall live.
That which foreign force has seized
We by sword shall retrieve.

March, march Dabrowski!
From Italy to our Polish land.
Let us now unite the nation
Under thy command.

Cross the Vistula, Cross the Warta,
We'll be Poles forever.
Following Bonaparte's example
We will yet prevail.
March, March Dabrowski!
(chorus)

THE FIRST POLISH SONG *to be treated as a national anthem was the 13th Century hymn, Bogurodzica (The Mother of God) which was very popular and sung by Polish knights before the battle of Grunwald. In the 18th Century the last Polish king, Stanislaw August Poniatowski tried to establish a new anthem but failed to make a national impact. Only the song of the Polish Legions became a real national anthem.*

When Napoleon created the Duchy of Warsaw in 1807, hopes rose once more and Dabrowski's Mazurek was very popular.

It was at this time that he was presented with an embroidered flag, made by his wife, Barbara Chlapowska, with the motto "Za wolnosz wasze i nasze" (For your freedom and ours.) The Duchy didn't last but Wybicki's song did and in 1926 it was officially proclaimed the national emblem of Poland.

In 1976, it was once more proclaimed the national anthem of the Polish People's Republic.

PISANKI, KRASANKI

In a certain day, long, long ago, a Cyrean peddler was on his way to the marketplace with a basket of eggs to sell. When he entered the town, he came upon an angry crowd. They were mocking a man, staggering beneath the weight of a heavy wooden cross.

Roman soldiers were swearing, dogs were barking, women were weeping; all stood by, watching as the man struggled, with sand and dust burning into his fresh cuts and bruises.

"What is this?" he murmured. Taking pity on the man, he put down his basket of eggs and ran to help him carry the heavy load.

Much later, when he returned to his basket, he found the entire basket of eggs had been transformed into all the colors of the rainbow. Simon, the Cyreanian, was astonished.

When Christ was nailed to the cross, his mother stood by, her heart heavy with grief. Finally, she could endure it no longer. In desperation, she went to the Palace with the basket of eggs. As she pleaded with Pontius Pilate, her tears fell on the eggs and they formed dots of brilliant color. To this day, the dots are called Our Lady's Tears.

FROM ANCIENT CHINA TO PERSIA, *from Rome to Athens, eggs were exchanged at annual spring festivals, with wishes of immortality and fertility. The Romans and Greeks often buried eggs with their dead, or left a basket of eggs on their tombs. Dyed red, a symbol of mourning, it probably was the origin of the tradition of decorating eggs at Easter time.*

In archaeological digs in Opole, eggs shaped from clay were unearthed from under ancient dwellings of the tenth Century.

In Gdansk, eggs made from limestone were found, all of them with various ornaments and painted or etched with a burin. It is thought that such eggs had been placed under the thresholds of the homes in an offering to the protective spirits of the household. Eggs, symbolic of the mystery of life, became the symbol of resurrection and victory of life over death.

Decorated eggs in Poland are usually found in two styles. The simplest, kraszanki, are usually produced in the western part of Poland and they are boiled and dyed in one color. At times an outline of a bird, flower or animal is drawn, by scratching out some of the color.

Pisanki, the batiked eggs, are artistic designs of many colors. They are usually raw, dipped into a dye, a design applied with a beeswax pen and dipped into another color. The process is repeated as often as the artist wishes. When completed, the beeswax is removed by placing it in a warm oven until the wax softens and can be rubbed off. A sight to behold.

Florence Waszkelewicz Clowes

THE MYSTERY OF THE BLACK MADONNA

People throughout Poland and indeed, throughout the world, come to pray before a most famous picture, the Miraculous Black Madonna of Czestochowa. Any Pole can tell you about their venerated Madonna and how it got to be in the cathedral of Jasna Gora.

It seems the painting was created on a cedar board by St. Luke the Evangelist, who according to tradition took the board from a table in the house of Joseph and Mary in Nazareth. This and the fact that St. Luke is said to have painted Our Lady and Child from life, makes the picture a holy relic surrounded by the greatest devotion.

During the Roman persecutions, the Christian community kept the painting hidden in the catacombs near the town of Pella. For three hundred years, it was revered by the faithful in and near Jerusalem.

Then, in 326 A.D., Helen, the mother of Constantine the Great, heard of the picture and decided she must have it for her son. With persuasion, she was able to locate and bring it to Constantinople.

Constantine, the first Christian emperor of Rome, built a church as a fitting setting for the picture, where it remained for the next five hundred years. Miracles attributed to the picture were continually being reported.

Once, when the Persians besieged the city, the Patriarch carried the icon to the city wall. At the sight of the image, the enemy retreated in fear.

Later on, Prince Leo of Ruthenia persuaded the Emperor to give the picture to him. The prince then enshrined it in a castle at Belz in Russia, where it remained for half a Century,

179

becoming a place of many pilgrimages.

In the fourteenth Century, Belz was conquered by Prince Wladystaw Opolczyk, who also constructed a special chamber to hold the portrait.

Tartars were constantly sweeping across the plains of Russia and into Poland and Hungary and one of these attacks was on the castle at Belz.

In the heat of the battle, an arrow shot from the bow of a Tartar warrior entered the chapel through a window and struck the sacred picture, leaving a scar on the throat of the Madonna. This so enraged Wladyslaw and his company that, with supernatural zeal, they saved the day from total defeat.

The constant Tartar attacks, however, caused Wladyslaw to consider moving the picture to a safer place. He decided on Opola and loaded the icon into a wagon and began the journey. It took him through the small town of Czestochowa, where he rested for the night.

The following morning the precious relic was reloaded into the wagon to continue the journey. To everyone's surprise, the horses could not, or would not, budge from the spot.

The Prince fell to his knees before the image, praying for guidance. His prayers were heard and he was convinced it was the will of God to permanently deposit the picture in Czestochowa, on the white limestone hill, Jasna Gora.

In solemn procession the picture was brought to the Church of the Assumption the 26th day of August, 1382. On that very day, he ordered a convent, church and cloister to be erected on the hill.

He brought a group of Pauline monks from Hungary, confiding the picture into their care, for they were considered the most pious and religious in all Europe. Sixteen white-robed friars soon arrived and for five and one half centuries, they have been connected with the history of the miraculous painting.

A relative calm settled over the shrine for many years. Pilgrimages and miraculous cures were constantly happening. The friars kept a record of it all.

Then, in 1430, the Hussites began attacking Czestochowa.

Murdering and plundering, they took the picture from the altar, preparing to carry it off as part of their loot. But the horses pulling their carts refused to go past the town limits. Infuriated, the soldiers began to throw goods off the cart to lighten the load. The icon was hurled to the ground with such force that it broke in three parts. One of the soldiers drew his saber and slashed the right cheek of the Virgin's face twice. Before he could strike again, he fell to the ground, dead. Seeing this, his companions fled in panic.

The icon was recovered and King Wladyslaw Jagiello ordered a major restoration and renovation to the cathedral. When completed, the picture was placed in the glorious cathedral with much pomp and ceremony, the people were convinced more than ever that the Mother of God was watching and protecting them. The fame of the miraculous picture spread rapidly. Public events immortalized the shrine and made it the center of national unity and prayer.

In the middle of the seventeenth Century, invaders once again poured into Poland from every side. During this "deluge" the King fled to Silesia and the people took refuge in forts and fortified monasteries. One of the last resisting monasteries was Czestochowa.

Two months before Christmas, 10,000 Swedish soldiers began laying siege on the monastery. The cannon balls, to the dismay and horror of the invaders, rebounded, killing many Swedes. The Virgin and Child were seen in the midst of the battle in a supernatural light; the enemy fled in panic. The whole Polish nation took courage at this unexpected victory, reaffirming their faith in the precious icon.

In 1656, King John Casimir proclaimed Mary Queen and Sovereign of Poland and vowed to devote the rest of his reign to establishing social justice for all.

Each morning as the sun rises in the east and warms the plains of southwestern Poland with its brilliant rays, the sounds of silver trumpets are heard at the shrine of Czestochowa. They announce to the world that the silver screen covering the famous Black Madonna is once more being lifted so all may see the precious icon.

MODERN TECHNIQUES, *of microscope, x-ray and technological analysis have helped establish some new facts about the miraculous painting.*

Rudolph Kozlowski, Chief Conservator at the State Art Collection at Wawel Castle made a study from 1948-52. His analysis points to the fact that the original Madonna was most likely painted in the ninth Century. The original picture was so damaged that in 1430 the painting was entirely redone and given a new backing and frame.

Clues exist, however, to point to the Early Byzantine or late Old Christian era. That painting was sized on a linden board and backed with cypress, used to repel bores. The sizing was a brown glue and the painting was done in an encaustic technique (color and wax fused by heat), which was not used in later centuries.

When Wladyslaw summoned Ruthenian painters to repair the shattered picture, they failed, for it was impossible to touch up an encaustic painting with the then prevalent method of distemper (glue or gum used as a binding agent). The paint ran and the scars on the Madonna's face could not be covered.

The scars had been made with a burin, not the legendary sword, and had to be touched up with cinnabar—a red pigment. The many nail holes in the old boards were made by the practice of nailing jewels, metal plates and dresses directly to the painting.

The painting itself is of Egypto-Hellenistic style. The eyes especially reveal the techniques used on the faces of Egyptian mummy portraits. They look directly forward and a side source of light makes the eyes seem alive and looking directly at you, no matter where you stand. After the fifteenth Century, artists directed the eyes sideways. The new portrait was sized with ground chalk, similar to that found in Chelm.

A frame was fitted precisely to the picture to give it strength and x-rays show few nail holes on the new canvas as objects were no longer attached directly to the picture. The crowns, dresses and jewels are kept away from it in order to preserve the painting. An exact copy of the original painting was made, including the scars.

In 1925-26 when Jan Rutkowski renovated the picture, he removed layers of accumulated dirt and soot from the robes. He didn't remove the darkened varnish from the face of the Madonna, for that was how the people knew the picture.

The Madonna and Child were originally white but the old varnish, darkened with age and soot from the thousands of smoking candles, had become known as the Black Madonna.

Mr. Kozlowski substantiates the fact that the painting originated in the early centuries, somewhere in the Jerusalem area and was revered long before it came to Poland.

Every Holy Thursday, the decorative dresses are interchanged with others. A gown of precious jewels, a second embroidered with golden beads and golden crowns add to the beauty and splendor of the Black Madonna, a symbol of the devotion and faith of the Polish people.

HOW KALISZ BEGAN

Two thousand years ago, or maybe even more, the land was covered with large ancient forests where wild beasts roamed. A river divided the area, with marshes and bogs on either side. One day, when the sun was just setting, a great noise echoed through the forest—the pounding of hooves, the snorting of animals and the shouts of people made a deafening sound.

Suddenly on a hillside, there appeared a powerful king of animals, the bison. It stopped as it reached the top, tired and breathing heavily, its head touching the ground, its great horns scraping the grass. Two arrows had been thrust into either side and a broken lance in his chest. Weakened, he tried to continue his flight but he fell to the ground, defeated at last.

The edge of the forest came alive with war cries—angry, excited howling voices, from three different directions. As they came upon the animal, they were surprised to see each other. Axes and lance in hand, they stared at the groups of warriors. These people, children of the children of Lech, Rus and Czech, began to fight each other for the bison and control of the hill. "Kali, kali, kali," they called. By the dark of the night, the Lechi gained control and the other groups fled into the forest.

The next day, the Lechi warriors looked the area over and liked what they saw. The mud and muck on the sides of the river would protect them from sudden attacks and the forest close by would provide them with firewood and housing. They settled a camp there and later built a fortress and planted oak trees around their growing town, which they decided to name KALI, after their screaming war cries.

KALISZ, ONE OF THE OLDEST *towns in Poland, was a market-place on the amber route from the Far East. Their coat of arms consists of a warrior alerting the town with a war cry from the bison's horn. Kali means mud and muck.*

COPERNICUS, FAUST AND TWARDOWSKI

At the time when Nicolaus Copernicus was a student at the University of Krakow, he often met with Pan Twardowski to review their scientific findings and with their friends, discussed the many things that were happening in Krakow and Europe. Other scientists were known to the Poles, such as Dr. George Faust, the German. He was considered one of the most famous wizards in Europe.

Faust had heard of the new ideas of Copernicus and was very eager to learn more. He also knew about the extraordinary magic that Pan Twardowski performed and wanted to talk with both of them personally. So he decided to visit Krakow. Once there, he went to an old tavern, Pukier on the Rynek, that Twardowski often visited.

This tavern was very well known, for even King Zygmunt Waza had visited it. The shop sold very good wines and drink and the innkeeper, Fukier, was jolly and always telling jokes and proverbs to his customers.

But when the King moved the capitol to Warsaw, things slowed down a bit. One of the proverbs that Fukier had written on the wall was:

"All prefer to have a better drink but your wallet won't allow it. Drink less today, so tomorrow you can drink like a king!"

Not everyone appreciated the proverb, for many came to the tavern to bury their sorrows and didn't care what happened tomorrow.

Faust entered the tavern, a dark-skinned stranger in dark, poor clothing and sat in a corner watching the activities. Soon Twardowski, a tall man with a mustache twirled up on the ends, in colorful ornate clothing arrived. He walked straight toward Faust and extended his hand. "Honored Dr. Faust, welcome! I am at your service."

Faust was surprised that Twardowski knew him and even seemed able to read his mind. But Twardowski was friendly and introduced him to others in the tavern and then called for drinks.

Soon Twardowski hit his glass with the stone in his beautiful ring and said, "I'd like to play some tricks but I'm afraid you can do better than I. No?"

Faust protested, "Oh no! In Krakow, like our learned academia, everyone knows Latin. Look, even the proverb on the wall! Everyone in Europe knows about the abilities of Twardowski! Please."

Others in the tavern joined them. One old *szlachta* who had been in the tavern all day also joined them.

A little tipsy, he pointed to the proverb. "Read the proverb," he called loudly.

"Today, I will live like a king. Drinks on the house," he called loudly.

Twardowski looked at the man, his eyes narrowed and a strange light shone from them. Leaning close to the nobleman, he softly blew in his ear then said, "Look, everyone, this nobleman sits on a King's throne," which had suddenly appeared at the table. "And the crown on his head grows larger by the minute." Indeed the nobleman could hardly keep his head up and called for others to help him hold the heavy crown.

Suddenly a spider came down from the ceiling, spinning a web to the crown, then proceeded to lift the crown up to the ceiling, where it disappeared behind the ornate ceiling beam. The throne disappeared and the man found himself sitting on the floor, in a drunken stupor. Everyone laughed with astonishment and delight.

They praised Twardowski and looked at Faust for his reaction.

Much impressed, Faust grasped Twardowski's hand. "Krakow is known as the Paris of the North but this is truly great magic! Who else among us can play tricks through the night?"

But the innkeeper protested. "I don't like black magic. I'm afraid of ghosts and talking to the devil. Please go to Twardowski's place. It is getting late."

Dr. Faust didn't listen to him and continued talking. "Don't you have another great wizard?" he asked. "A young student who studies the distant stars—an astrologer?"

Twardowski twirled his mustache. "Astrologer? What astrologer? Astrologers study the heavens and will tell your fortune by the stars. It is difficult work but many people find it useful. But if you—"

In walked Nicolaus Copernicus, who interrupted Twardowski's conversation. "What is this I hear about astrologers?"

Dr. Faust greeted Copernicus warmly, reached into his pocket for some gold coins and tossed them toward the innkeeper. He took the money and left them to their drink and talk about matters only they understood.

Twardowski continued where he had left off. "But if you want to know about Astronomy, do ask Nicolaus!"

"Yes," said Dr. Faust. "I have heard of your work in European universities and am very interested in your opinions, which I wish you would share with us but first I have a problem I would like to share with you.

"You are both familiar with the 'elixir of youth'," and he reached into his cloak and brought out a small weasel.

"You see, one half of him is young and strong. The other half old and shriveled. See, even his right eye is dull and sluggish."

Twardowski and Copernicus studied the animal. "Well, Twardowski finally replied, "I don't know how you created this dilemma but I recommend you bring it to the kitchen and put the young part on the grill and give the old part to the dogs. Then eat the young part."

"But what happens if the wrong part is cooked and eaten by mistake?" asked Nicolaus.

"Alas," sighed Faust, "Old. Suddenly very old."

"Well, we can't touch that wonder." Twardowski declared. "Polish noblemen won't eat water rats, even to make them young. Only eggs and kielbasa and other dainty tidbits."

Later, they left the tavern and went out into the dark starry night. The moon and stars shone brightly. Nicolaus stood under the clock tower and stared at the heavens.

"I would love to go to the top of the clock tower and study the skies."

"Well, let's do it," Twardowski quickly replied.

"Oh, the guards won't allow us to go up at night."

"Phoof!" Twardowski scoffed. "That's only a trifle. Let's go," and he threw some gold coins at the guards and entered the stairway to the tower, followed by others.

High above the town, the three learned men became mesmerized by the wonderful sight of the millions of stars and the moon twinkling in a blanket of blackness.

Finally Copernicus said, "All the heavenly bodies are like large and small balls, turning. The earth and moon are turning. Everything turns around a big flaming sun."

Faust didn't say anything but decided Nicolaus was right.

But Twardowski asked, "How come? The heavenly bodies supposedly have their own cycles. Why are they round?"

Copernicus only answered, "They were formed that way."

Twardowski hit his head with the palm of his hand. "Of course, you're right. My head is also round and everything is turning around,"—for he was beginning to feel the effects of the evening's drinks—"and a little bit of wine can give one a different view. I have to agree with you, Nicolaus."

Faust and Twardowski respected the new ideas of Copernicus. This great scientific statement, which was to shake the world, was first shared with Faust and Twardowski in Krakow.

NICOLAUS COPERNICUS, (1473-1543) was born in To-run, Poland and is considered the father of modern science. His book, De revolutionbus, On the Revolutions of the Heavenly Spheres, *suggested the sun was the center of the universe, not the earth. Approximately 950 books were published in two editions and over 600 still exist in universities and private collections throughout the world.*

THE BREAD OF OLIWA

In the year of our Lord, 1217, a great famine developed in the land around Gdansk. The people were weary and hungry, trying to find food for all the townspeople. In the nearby village of Oliwa, there was a Cistercian convent, a monastery and a beautiful church. The priests baked bread and sold it to the townspeople as a means to support themselves.

When there was no food to be found in Gdansk, the townspeople went begging to the convent. The devout abbot was concerned and told his brothers to give each person a loaf of bread.

The people were very grateful, as each received its portion. But one peasant, who had received his bread, returned to the convent and stood in line for another loaf. He sobbed and begged for bread, saying he had a sick child at home and couldn't find anything for him to eat. The abbot gave him another loaf of bread.

On the road home, he suddenly came upon a woman with a small child in her arms. "Please," she said. "We are so weary. Can we have some of your bread?"

The peasant, who was carrying his bread under his cloak was surprised. He didn't think anyone could see the bread. Reaching in his cloak to touch the bread, making sure it was there, he said, "I don't have any bread."

"What is that lump under your cloak?"

"This is only a stone I am carrying," and he poked at the hidden loaf.

"Oh, really," the woman said in surprise. "Then let it be only a stone," and she disappeared as suddenly as she had appeared.

The peasant continued on his way. When he reached home, he gleefully took out the bread but it was no longer bread.

It was a stone loaf, with the indent of his finger in one side. He became frightened and wondered who the woman was. Quickly he returned to Oliwa and confessed all to the abbot.

"My son," the abbot sighed. "You have been punished by Our Lady for your selfishness. I will place this stone on the altar to remind you of your sins and for all to see!" And there it is to this day.

OLIWA, A SMALL *settlement by the sea, is a suburb of Gdansk. At the time of this legend, Europe was beginning to feel the start of miseries to come. The fourteenth Century brought about the Little Ice Age and the Black Death plague that swept through Europe.*

SEDZIWOJ AND SETON IN KRAKOW

In the sixteenth Century, there was great excitement among the learned men in Krakow. News spread that Alexander Seton, who was studying in Europe, had discovered the secret to the philosopher's stone. The alchemist from Scotland lectured in the great universities but soon was imprisoned by the Electors from Dresden who wanted him to reveal the secret. They craved the secret for changing base metals and liquids into gold, the dream of every man. The prince of the Saxon dynasty was angry with Seton and commanded him put on the torture rack until he revealed his secret. But the alchemist kept the mysterious formula to himself.

This news from Dresden soon reached Krakow. The great Marshal Wolski, (who had at another time offered the Camoldolite fathers the white silver mountain for their monastery, later called Bielany), arrived at the home of the well-known alchemist Michael Sedziwoj.

He knew Sedziwoj was a friend of Seton's since Sedziwoj prepared powders for the guilders, priests and alchemists throughout the country. Wolski was known as a patron of the arts and literature and he himself tested recipes for guilders, dyers and painters.

"Sedziwoj," Wolski said, "I want you to go to Dresden and save Seton. He won't last much longer under torture and the secret of the philosopher's stone will be lost forever. You can have all the money that you need.

And so it was that Sedziwoj went off to rescue Seton. Dressed in nobleman's clothing and throwing money around, he was able to convince the torturers to at least place Seton in a dry cell and to give him more food. He convinced the prince that he would be able to extract the secret from Seton if he were able to talk to him.

In the process of bribing the prison guards, Sedziwoj befriended the commander's daughter. She began to do small favors for him. When Sedziwoj decided to throw a large party, she helped him. Sedziwoj invited everyone—the commander of the prison and all the guards.

Everyone was having a good time, drinking and eating and joking. The young daughter helped Sedziwoj serve beer to them all. But the Pole didn't drink at all, whereas the Germans one after other slipped off their benches, unconscious and fell into a deep sleep.

No one knew of the drug the alchemist had dropped into the casks of beer that the commander's daughter was serving! The feast lasted well into the evening.

Before morning light, Sedziwoj was heading for the Polish border with Seton. The Saxon prince, outraged at being duped, went after him but it was too late. Sedziwoj had already reached the border and sent word ahead to spread the news. He entered the suburb of Lobzowa where crowds of people—guilders, standard-bearers and noblemen greeted him with great joy.

Sedziwoj brought the weak master to his home near Kanonicz street and placed him in luxurious surroundings. The doctors of Krakow, the best in the kingdom, spent whole days at his bedside, treating his wounds. King Zygmunt III, Emperor Rudolph and other heads of state were concerned about his health as news of his condition spread. All were curious about Seton's secret and they waited weeks and months as he struggled for his life.

One evening as golden rays of the setting sun flooded the window, Seton spoke to his rescuer. "My dear friend and pupil, I am grateful to you for saving my life, you show the faith of humankind. Now I will not die as a criminal. The Electors in Nuremberg tortured others—Witt Stwosz—the same as me, for the secret of making gold. I owe my life to you but I can't give you my secret."

"Master, don't worry. When you regain your health, we will study together."

"No, we won't. My body is rotting away. Look at my wounds. They don't heal. I will die soon." He took out a small elephant tusk, which he had managed to keep with him this whole time.

"Here," he said. "Gold water. Here is the tincture, no more than two ounces! Use it sparingly, guard it with your life. You are well protected by the kings and Marshal Wolski. For scholars like us, learning and knowledge are of greater value than gold. From your studies, you will learn the secret. If I reveal it to you, you won't have the pleasure of discovering it for yourself. I didn't reveal it to the torturers who were trying to kill me everyday. I can't break my vow now."

The next day, the funeral bells rang throughout Krakow. Seton was buried in a Krakow church, along with the Kings of old but no one knows where, for mysteriously his body and marker have disappeared.

Sedziwoj went to work with enthusiasm. He was determined to learn more of the composition of the gold-water. Each test and experiment took much time and very costly drops of tincture. He neglected his own work. His resources were dwindling.

Finally, he made an appearance before King Zygmunt III and his courtly entourage where he successfully transformed three silver coins into gold. (This scene is portrayed in a painting by Jan Matejko.)

The King rewarded Sedziwoj lavishly and encouraged him to further research. He then demanded a transformation of metal to gold to support the funding of his many troops but Sedziwoj was unable to perform the task again.

Everyone, kings, professors, noblemen and even women dreamed about synthesizing metal into gold, gunpowder into gold, everything into gold.

Sedziwoj learned many things but he still did not obtain the full formula. In desperation, he decided to marry Seton's widow.

His wife and two of their four children had died several years ago and to tell the truth, he badly needed a wife, for he was so obsessed with his work, he took little care of his home or clothing. Once he was married, he was able to study all of Seton's manuscripts and formulas. Even with this information, he could not unlock Seton's secret.

He discovered many things and his treatises on alchemy were translated into many languages and read throughout Europe. Finally, in a firm manner, he announced "Thus far, my research on the philosopher's stone have been unsuccessful. I can do no more!"

IN MEDIEVAL TIMES *alchemy was a serious study. Sedziwoj was a courier to Emperor Rudolph II and King Sigismund III. He participated in many alchemy studies with his friends. Mysterious and intriguing, he was undoubtedly a double agent.*

His De lapide philosophorum *was of great value for the history of science. Besides formulas for the philosopher's stone, it contained interesting notes concerning the components of air. It contained the first idea of the existence of "invisible niter"—oxygen.*

Sedziwoj, latinized as Sendivogius, has now changed to Sedzimir. Today, there is a firm founded in the United States by the late Tadeusz Sedzimir, inventor, scientist and philanthropist.

Scottish alchemist Alexander Seton studied in Dresden in the seventeenth Century.

THE TALE OF THE MOON

Long, long ago two old women lived beside a lovely lake, deep in the Sudety mountains. They lived next to each other, each in their own little cottage. The cottages were very old, with log walls and thatched roofs and brightly painted window sills full of bright flowers.

People in the distant villages called them "the two Babcias"—grandmothers.

The babcias loved the peace and quiet of the forest, picking berries in the fields and mushrooms in the forest. They raised their own vegetables in small garden plots. But they were as different as night and day.

One babcia, Dobabcia, was good, kind and generous, sharing all she had with the villagers who came to visit.

But the other, Bababcia, was always grumbling about something. She was stingy and jealous of everything and everyone.

One evening Dobabcia went for a walk down the silvery moonlit path to the lake. She was startled by the moon's reflection in the lake. Looking up to the heavens, she called, "Mr. Moon, why are you so thin? You're all bent over like a curved needle. Don't you have anything to eat? You look starved!"

"No," he said. "I haven't eaten for quite a few days. And I am hungry. Everyone wants me to do my job, shining brightly but no one will give me anything to eat."

"Oh, Mr. Moon, I will give you something to eat. Come visit me before you leave the heavens. This path leads right to my door." Saying that, Dobabcia returned home to prepare a meal for him.

Later that night Bababcia saw a strange light coming from her neighbor's window. It looked like a bright silvery lantern. What could that be, she asked herself.

She crept over to her neighbor's cottage and looked in the window. Mr. Moon was sitting at the table, pale and lean but with a wonderful glow about him. His clothing sparkled and twinkled with silver shots of light.

Bababcia could see a bowl of pierogi swimming in butter, a pitcher of milk and a loaf of bread on the colorful tablecloth. A jar of honey stood near a glass of tea. Fresh blueberries were sprinkled with sugar.

The moon was smiling happily as Dobabcia urged him to eat more and more. When he could eat no more, they went outside into the cool night and sat on the doorstep for a while.

Bababcia ran home before they could see her peeking in the window.

Finally he rose and said, "I must go now, it's almost daylight. Thank you so much for your hospitality."

"Please come back tomorrow and we'll have another late supper," Dobabcia urged.

The moon nodded and off he went down the silvery path to the lake. There he quickly glided into the heavens.

The following night Bababcia again looked out of her window and saw the moon visiting her neighbor. They were enjoying a nice late supper. Bababcia shut her eyes to the sight and went to bed, grumbling and jealous. She hadn't been invited to have supper with them.

Every night the moon visited his friend and he began to look a little fatter. He would pat his stomach with content as he left. In a week he went from a sliver of a crescent to a half-round moon. His light grew brighter in the heavens.

By the following week he was full and round and shining brightly in the dark heavens.

Bababcia was seized with envy and began to mumble, "Why does the pretty moon visit my neighbor and not me?" She decided to find out and went the lake that night.

"Hey, Mr. Moon," she called. "You have been visiting my neighbor for two weeks now. How about visiting me for two weeks? That would be fair, wouldn't it?"

"Will you give me something to eat if I'm hungry?" asked the moon.

"I will."

"Promise?"

"I promise, if you promise to visit me," answered Bababcia. And the moon spun around and promised.

For the next week he visited Bababcia and ate supper with her. But she didn't serve him very much and it wasn't long before he started to slim down. His round figure shrunk in half.

In the following week he grew even thinner. Bababcia was so stingy with her servings that the moon soon became completely curved over and shrunken up.

Dobabcia saw what was happening at her friends' home so she called to the moon, "Mr. Moon, come and visit me again. I have some nice pastries."

The moon was grateful for such a generous friend who was willing to share all she had. Over the next two weeks she gave him plenty to eat, urging him to have more. He grew stronger and brighter until finally he was full and round once more.

In that way Mr. Moon changed, getting fat and round and then, once again a sliver of himself, month after month, year after year. If you don't believe me, look in the heavens, see the moon for yourself and guess who is feeding him.

THIS TALE WAS FOUND *in children's school books in Kielce. It introduces them to the four stages of the moon— Waxing Crescent to a half-moon, Waxing Gibbons to a full moon, Waning Crescent to a half-moon, followed by a Waning Gibbons to another cycle with a New Moon.*

Bibliography

Archacki, Henry. "Pre-historic Fortress-settlement built near Biskupin." Zgoda. December, 1980.

Anstruther, Fay C. Old Polish Legends, Retold. Glascow: Polish Library, 1945.

Baring-Gould, S. Curious Myths of the Middle Ages. London: Longmans, Green & Co., 1906.

Barroclough, Geoffry, ed. Eastern and Western Europe in the Middle Ages. New York: Harcourt, 1970.

Bukowska-Gedigowa, Janina. Wczesnosrednio-Wieczny Grod Na Ostroku w Opolu. Polskiej Akademia Nauk, 1986.

Benes, V.L. and N.G. Pounds. Poland. New York: Praeger Press, 1970.

Bocharski, Alexander, tr. "Biary Orzel." Plomyczek. December, 1972.

Bogucki, Peter. "A Glimpse of Iron Age Poland." Archeology. Sept/Oct, 1990.

Bogucki, Peter and Ryszard Grygiel. "Early Farmers of the North European Plain." Scientific American. April, 1983.

Budrewicz, Olgied. Poland For Beginners. Warsaw: Interpress Publishers, 1980.

Chwolewik, Witold. comp. Panstwowe Wydawn Naukowe. Warsaw: 1968.

Coleman, Marion. The Man On The Moon. Cheshire, CT: Cherry Hill Books, 1971.

Coleman, Marion. A Brigand, Two Queens and a Prankster. Cheshire, Cherry Hill Books, 1972.

DeBary, William, comp. Sources of Chinese Tradition. New York: Columbia University Press, 1970.

Dorson, Richard. Folktales Told Around The World. Chicago: University of Chicago Press 1975.

Dzieciol, Witold. The Origins of Poland. London: Veritasa Foundation Publications, 1963.

Frazer, Edward. The Golden Bough, A Study of Magic and Religion. New York: Macmillan, 1951.

Heyduk, Bronislaw. Legendy i Opowiesci O Krakowie. Wroclaw: Wydawnictwo Literackie, Krakow, 1985.

Iaggard. The World, Historical Descriptions of the Most Famous Kingdoms and Commonwealths. London, 1601.

Jarecka, Louise. Made in Poland. New York: Alfred Knoff, 1949.

Jasienica, Pawel. Piast Poland. New York; American Institute of Polish Culture, Hippocrene Books, 1985.

Kelly, Eric. The Land and People of Poland. Philadelphia: Lippincott, 1964.

Kelly, Eric. Polish Legends and Tales. New York: Polish Publications Society of America, 1971.

Kor-Walczak, Eligiusz. Basnie i Legendy Kaliskie. Poznan: Wydawnictwo Poznanskie, 1986.

Kruszewska, A and M. Coleman. "The Wanda Theme in Polish Literature and Life." American Slavic and East European Review, May 1947.

Krzyzanowski, Julian. Slownik Folkloru Polskiego. Warsaw: Wiedza Powszechna, 1965.

Leciejewicza, Lecha. Maly Stownik Kultury Dawnych Stowian. Warsaw: Wiedza Powszechna, 1972.

Milosz, Czeslaw. The History of Polish Literature. New York: Macmillan, 1969.

Orion, Maian and Jan Tyszkiewicz. Legendy i Podania Polskie. Warsaw: Wydawnietwo PTTK, 1986.

Peterson, Roger. "White Storks Vanishing Sentinels of the Rooftops." National Geographic, June, 1962.

Porazinska, Janina. "Starodzieje". Warsaw: Nasza Ksiegarnia, 1964.

Ruland, Wilhelm. The Finest Legends of the Rhine. Germany, 1902.

Siemienska, Lucjan. Podania i Legendy Polskie, Ruskie i Litewski. Warsaw: Panstwowy Institut Wydawnieczy, 1975.

Simpson, Jacqueline. European Mythology. New York: Peter Bedrick Books, 1987.

Uminski, Sigmund. Tales of Early Poland. Detroit: Endurance Press, 1968.

Zajaczkowski, Wiestaw. Biskupin, Rezerwat Archeoloqiczny. Poznan: Wydawnictwo Poznanskie, 1987.